William Shakespeare's

A Midsummer Nights Dream
In Plain and Simple English

A SwipeSpeare™ Book
www.SwipeSpeare.com

Table of Contents

About This Series

The "SwipeSpeare™" series started as a way of telling Shakespeare for the modern reader—being careful to preserve the themes and integrity of the original. Visit our website SwipeSpeare.com to see other books in the series, as well as the interactive, and swipe-able, app!

The series is expanding every month. Visit BookCaps.com to see non-Shakespeare books in this series, and while you are there join the Facebook page, so you are first to know when a new book comes out.

Characters

THESEUS, Duke of Athens.

EGEUS, Father to Hermia.

LYSANDER, in love with Hermia.

DEMETRIUS, in love with Hermia.

PHILOSTRATE, Master of the Revels to Theseus.

QUINCE, the Carpenter.

SNUG, the Joiner.

BOTTOM, the Weaver.

FLUTE, the Bellows-mender.

SNOUT, the Tinker.

STARVELING, the Tailor.

HIPPOLYTA, Queen of the Amazons, bethrothed to Theseus.

HERMIA, daughter to Egeus, in love with Lysander.

HELENA, in love with Demetrius.

OBERON, King of the Fairies.

TITANIA, Queen of the Fairies.

PUCK, or ROBIN GOODFELLOW, a Fairy.

PEASBLOSSOM, Fairy.

COBWEB, Fairy.

MOTH, Fairy.

MUSTARDSEED, Fairy.

PYRAMUS, THISBE, WALL, MOONSHINE, LION, Characters in the Interlude performed by the Clowns.

Other Fairies attending their King and Queen. Attendants on Theseus and Hippolyta.

Act I

Scene I

The palace of THESEUS.

Enter THESEUS, HIPPOLYTA, PHILOSTRATE, and Attendants

THESEUS
Now, fair Hippolyta, our nuptial hour
Draws on apace; four happy days bring in
Another moon: but, O, methinks, how slow
This old moon wanes! she lingers my desires,
Like to a step-dame or a dowager
Long withering out a young man revenue.

*My dear Hippolyta, our wedding day
Is coming soon, in exactly four days, when there
is a new moon: but too slowly
is this moon waning! It is making me wait
anxiously, Like a step-mother or a widow
makes a son wait for his inheritance.*

HIPPOLYTA
Four days will quickly steep themselves in
night;
Four nights will quickly dream away the time;
And then the moon, like to a silver bow
New-bent in heaven, shall behold the night
Of our solemnities.

*But four days will quickly become four nights,
And we will dream through the four nights,
And then the new moon, shaped like a silver bow
Pulled back in the sky, will look at the night
That marks the day of our marriage.*

THESEUS
Go, Philostrate,
Stir up the Athenian youth to merriments;
Awake the pert and nimble spirit of mirth;
Turn melancholy forth to funerals;
The pale companion is not for our pomp.

*Go, Philostrate,
And get the young people of Athens to party.
Wake up the city with an air of celebration
And allow sadness only for funerals –
We do not need it mixed with our joy and
festivities.*

Exit PHILOSTRATE

Hippolyta, I woo'd thee with my sword,
And won thy love, doing thee injuries;
But I will wed thee in another key,
With pomp, with triumph and with revelling.

*Hippolyta, I courted you by sword in battle
And won your love as I defeated and kidnapped
you – But our wedding will be different,
celebratory, triumphant, and joyful.*

*Enter EGEUS, HERMIA, LYSANDER, and
DEMETRIUS*

EGEUS
Happy be Theseus, our renowned duke!

I hope you are well, Duke Theseus!

THESEUS

Thanks, good Egeus: what's the news with thee?

Thank you, Egeus

EGEUS
Full of vexation come I, with complaint
Against my child, my daughter Hermia.
Stand forth, Demetrius. My noble lord,
This man hath my consent to marry her.
Stand forth, Lysander: and my gracious duke,
This man hath bewitch'd the bosom of my child;
Thou, thou, Lysander, thou hast given her
rhymes,
And interchanged love-tokens with my child:
Thou hast by moonlight at her window sung,
With feigning voice verses of feigning love,
And stolen the impression of her fantasy
With bracelets of thy hair, rings, gawds,
conceits,
Knacks, trifles, nosegays, sweetmeats,
messengers
Of strong prevailment in unharden'd youth:
With cunning hast thou filch'd my daughter's
heart,
Turn'd her obedience, which is due to me,
To stubborn harshness: and, my gracious duke,
Be it so she; will not here before your grace
Consent to marry with Demetrius,
I beg the ancient privilege of Athens,
As she is mine, I may dispose of her:
Which shall be either to this gentleman
Or to her death, according to our law
Immediately provided in that case.

I am confused and worried for
Hermia, my daughter and child.
Come forward, Demetrius. My Lord,
I have agreed to this man marrying her.
Come forward, Lysander: and good duke,
This man has tricked my daughter's heart.
You, Lysander, you have written her poems,
And given her trinkets and gifts:
At night, below her window, you sang to her,
Deceiving her with insincere lyrics of untrue
love,
And have stirred her imagination
With locks of hair, rings, toys, favors,
Knickknacks, charms, flowers, and desserts,
convincing
Signs to strongly sway a naive youth.
Sneakily you have stolen my daughter's love,
So that she obeys you instead of me, and to me
Acts stubbornly and rudely. And now, gracious
duke,
I ask that you let me, if she will not here
Agree to marrying Demetrius,
Do what I am allowed as an Athenian father,
Who owns his daughter, and send her away:
Either to marry Demetrius,
Or to die, according to the law.

THESEUS
What say you, Hermia? be advised fair maid:
To you your father should be as a god;
One that composed your beauties, yea, and one
To whom you are but as a form in wax
By him imprinted and within his power
To leave the figure or disfigure it.
Demetrius is a worthy gentleman.

Well, Hermia – how do you respond? Know
this: Your father should be thought of as your
god – He created you, as beautiful as you are,
and So you are only a wax model
That he has signed as the artist, and as such
He may leave it untouched, or demolish it.
Demetrius is well worth marrying.

HERMIA
So is Lysander.

But Lysander is as well.

THESEUS
In himself he is;

Yes, outside of this situation he is,

But in this kind, wanting your father's voice,
The other must be held the worthier.

HERMIA
I would my father look'd but with my eyes.

THESEUS
Rather your eyes must with his judgment look.

HERMIA
I do entreat your grace to pardon me.
I know not by what power I am made bold,
Nor how it may concern my modesty,
In such a presence here to plead my thoughts;
But I beseech your grace that I may know
The worst that may befall me in this case,
If I refuse to wed Demetrius.

THESEUS
Either to die the death or to abjure
For ever the society of men.
Therefore, fair Hermia, question your desires;
Know of your youth, examine well your blood,
Whether, if you yield not to your father's choice,
You can endure the livery of a nun,
For aye to be in shady cloister mew'd,
To live a barren sister all your life,
Chanting faint hymns to the cold fruitless moon.
Thrice-blessed they that master so their blood,
To undergo such maiden pilgrimage;
But earthlier happy is the rose distill'd,
Than that which withering on the virgin thorn
Grows, lives and dies in single blessedness.

HERMIA
So will I grow, so live, so die, my lord,
Ere I will my virgin patent up
Unto his lordship, whose unwished yoke
My soul consents not to give sovereignty.

THESEUS
Take time to pause; and, by the nest new moon--
The sealing-day betwixt my love and me,
For everlasting bond of fellowship—
Upon that day either prepare to die

*But considering your father's opinion
Demetrius is the better man.*

I wish my father could see this as I do!

No, you should instead see it as he does.

*Please forgive me for what I am going to say.
I do not know how I feel so confident to speak
honestly, or how much I am overstepping my
place and being ill-mannered, And bring my
case to you who are my authority; But I ask,
because I wish to know for sure, What is the
worst that might happen to me If I refuse to
marry Demetrius?*

*You must either die or be banished
From marrying and sent to a nunnery.
So, beautiful Hermia, step back and search
yourself, Understand your immaturity, your
youth, and your temperament, So you can know,
if you do not obey your father, If you can live the
rest of your life as a nun. You would be caged in
a dark convent All your life, living as a nun,
childless, Chanting hymns to the cold moon,
which like you is without child. Believe me,
those that can quell their desires are blessed
triple For journeying through life as a nun is
admirable – But on this earth, it is happier to be
married, like a rose perfume, Rather than the
rose that on the same stem Grows, lives, and
dies, alone but chaste and blessed.*

*So I will likewise grow, live, and die alone, my
lord Before I consent to losing my virginity
To Demetrius, whose bond of marriage I do not
wish And to whose authority my soul does not
desire to bow.*

*Take time and think about your decision until
the new moon — which is when Hippolyta and I
will marry and be forever joined together –
And then you must be ready to die*

For disobedience to your father's will,
Or else to wed Demetrius, as he would;
Or on Diana's altar to protest
For aye austerity and single life.

For disobeying your father's will,
Or ready to wed Demetrius, as your father
wishes, Or like the chaste Roman goddess
Diana, commit Yourself to the nun's vows of
lifelong celibacy.

DEMETRIUS
Relent, sweet Hermia: and, Lysander, yield
Thy crazed title to my certain right.

Change your mind, sweet Hermia! And
Lysander, give up Your claim to the woman I am
due to marry.

LYSANDER
You have her father's love, Demetrius;
Let me have Hermia's: do you marry him.

Demetrius, you can have her father's love
And I can have Hermia's – why don't you marry
him?

EGEUS
Scornful Lysander! true, he hath my love,
And what is mine my love shall render him.
And she is mine, and all my right of her
I do estate unto Demetrius.

Rude Lysander! Yes, I love Demetrius,
And so I will give him what is mine:
My daughter, and the right to marry her
Is so allowed to Demetrius.

LYSANDER
I am, my lord, as well derived as he,
As well possess'd; my love is more than his;
My fortunes every way as fairly rank'd,
If not with vantage, as Demetrius';
And, which is more than all these boasts can be,
I am beloved of beauteous Hermia:
Why should not I then prosecute my right?
Demetrius, I'll avouch it to his head,
Made love to Nedar's daughter, Helena,
And won her soul; and she, sweet lady, dotes,
Devoutly dotes, dotes in idolatry,
Upon this spotted and inconstant man.

You know, sir, I come from as good a family as
he does, I am just as rich, and I love Hermia
more. In everything I rank just as highly,
If not higher, than Demetrius,
And moreover, which should be what is most
important, Beautiful Hermia loves me in return:
Why should I not be able to marry her?
Demetrius, I promise this is true,
Wooed Nedar's daughter, Helena,
Until she fell for him, and she, poor girl, loves,
Loves deeply, almost to the point of obsession,
This flawed and inconsistent man.

THESEUS
I must confess that I have heard so much,
And with Demetrius thought to have spoke
thereof;
But, being over-full of self-affairs,
My mind did lose it. But, Demetrius, come;
And come, Egeus; you shall go with me,
I have some private schooling for you both.
For you, fair Hermia, look you arm yourself
To fit your fancies to your father's will;
Or else the law of Athens yields you up--
Which by no means we may extenuate--
To death, or to a vow of single life.

Admittedly, I have heard similar rumors
And even considered speaking directly to
Demetrius about them,
But, being so busy with my own obligations
Forgot about it. Demetrius, come with me,
And you, Egeus, come with me as well:
I have some words in private to share with you
both. As for you, Hermia, prepare yourself
To do whatever your father's will commands,
Or else you must go before the Athenian Law –
From which we cannot save you –
And either die or become a nun.

Come, my Hippolyta: what cheer, my love?
Demetrius and Egeus, go along:
I must employ you in some business
Against our nuptial and confer with you
Of something nearly that concerns yourselves.

EGEUS
With duty and desire we follow you.

LYSANDER
How now, my love! why is your cheek so pale?
How chance the roses there do fade so fast?

HERMIA
Belike for want of rain, which I could well
Beteem them from the tempest of my eyes.

LYSANDER
Ay me! for aught that I could ever read,
Could ever hear by tale or history,
The course of true love never did run smooth;
But, either it was different in blood,--

HERMIA
O cross! too high to be enthrall'd to low.

LYSANDER
Or else misgraffed in respect of years,-

HERMIA
O spite! too old to be engaged to young.

LYSANDER
Or else it stood upon the choice of friends,--

HERMIA
O hell! to choose love by another's eyes.

LYSANDER
Or, if there were a sympathy in choice,
War, death, or sickness did lay siege to it,
Making it momentary as a sound,
Swift as a shadow, short as any dream;
Brief as the lightning in the collied night,

Come, Hippolyta – how are you, my love?
Demetrius and Egeus, come with us.
I must as you about something
Regarding my wedding, and speak with you
About something that concerns both of you.

We follow in order to obey, and because we
want to hear your words.

Exeunt all but LYSANDER and HERMIA

Oh Hermia, what is wrong? Why are you pale?
How did the rosy redness of your cheeks fade
away so quickly?

Like roses, my cheeks need rain, which I could
Give them by crying a storm upon them.

Oh no! But listen: everything I have read,
Either in fairy tale or true history,
Says true love must always overcome problems:
Sometimes the problem is being from different
classes--

How horrible to be so wealthy and in love with
someone so poor!

And sometimes there was a great age difference-

How awful to be so old and marrying someone
so young!

And sometimes the lovers' friends were against
the match--

How hellish to have to love only whom someone
else chose!

And sometimes, if the match was a good one,
War or death or illness attacked it
And ended it, as transient as a sound becoming
silent, As quick as a shadow disappearing, as
short as a dream upon waking, As brief as a

That, in a spleen, unfolds both heaven and earth,
And ere a man hath power to say 'Behold!'
The jaws of darkness do devour it up:
So quick bright things come to confusion.

HERMIA
If then true lovers have been ever cross'd,
It stands as an edict in destiny:
Then let us teach our trial patience,
Because it is a customary cross,
As due to love as thoughts and dreams and sighs,
Wishes and tears, poor fancy's followers.

LYSANDER
A good persuasion: therefore, hear me, Hermia.
I have a widow aunt, a dowager
Of great revenue, and she hath no child:
From Athens is her house remote seven leagues;
And she respects me as her only son.
There, gentle Hermia, may I marry thee;
And to that place the sharp Athenian law
Cannot pursue us. If thou lovest me then,
Steal forth thy father's house to-morrow night;
And in the wood, a league without the town,
Where I did meet thee once with Helena,
To do observance to a morn of May,
There will I stay for thee.

HERMIA
My good Lysander!
I swear to thee, by Cupid's strongest bow,
By his best arrow with the golden head,
By the simplicity of Venus' doves,
By that which knitteth souls and prospers loves,
And by that fire which burn'd the Carthage queen,
When the false Troyan under sail was seen,
By all the vows that ever men have broke,
In number more than ever women spoke,
In that same place thou hast appointed me,
To-morrow truly will I meet with thee.

LYSANDER
Keep promise, love. Look, here comes Helena

lightning strike in the black night sky That at once shows the earth and the sky And, before a man can say "Look!" Is gone into darkness, as if swallowed. Thus, good and bright things may quickly change.

Then it seems that true lovers are so often troubled That fighting obstacles is their fate. So we should be patient in this trial Because it is just as normal of a problem For lovers as thoughts, dreams, sighs Wishes, and tears – all things that accompany love.

I agree, Hermia, now listen: I have a widowed aunt Who is very wealthy and has no child for her inheritance. She lives far from Athens And loves me like a son. We should thus, gentle Hermia, go there to wed, Because that far away the Athenian Law Has no effect. So, if you love me, Run away from your father's house tomorrow night And go to the forest, a mile outside of town, To the place where I once met Helena And watched the sunrise one May: I will wait for you there.

Oh good Lysander! I promise, by the bow of Cupid, messenger of Love, By his best arrow with a golden tip, By Venus' doves which are simple and pure, By the fates that tie lovers together and gives them success, And by the fire that the Carthage queen burned herself in When her lover from Troy left by the sea, By all the promises that men have broken Which far outnumber the promises women made, In the place that you have told me to go Will I be, tomorrow, to see you.

Keep your word, love. Look, here comes Helena.

HERMIA
God speed fair Helena! whither away?

Enter HELENA

Enter HELENA

Greetings beautiful Helena! Where are you going?

HELENA
Call you me fair? that fair again unsay.
Demetrius loves your fair: O happy fair!
Your eyes are lode-stars; and your tongue's sweet air
More tuneable than lark to shepherd's ear,
When wheat is green, when hawthorn buds appear.
Sickness is catching: O, were favour so,
Yours would I catch, fair Hermia, ere I go;
My ear should catch your voice, my eye your eye,
My tongue should catch your tongue's sweet melody.
Were the world mine, Demetrius being bated,
The rest I'd give to be to you translated.
O, teach me how you look, and with what art
You sway the motion of Demetrius' heart.

*You call me beautiful? Well don't:
Demetrius prefers your beauty – oh, that is the best beauty! Your eyes are like bright stars and your voice Is more pleasing than the songbird is to the shepherd In Springtime when the wheat is still green and the flower buds first appear.
I feel sick: if only a lover's preference were like sickness, Then I could catch Demetrius's favor from you, fair Helena, before I leave.
Your voice would infect my ear and my eyes would become as yours,
My voice as sweet and melodious as your voice.
Were everything in the world mine except Demetrius,
I would give it to you just to be changed into you. Teach me how you create your beauty and how You captured Demetrius's eye and favor.*

HERMIA
I frown upon him, yet he loves me still.

I never smile at him, I only frown, but it has no effect: he loves me still.

HELENA
O that your frowns would teach my smiles such skill!

I wish I could teach my smiles how to be as alluring as your frowns!

HERMIA
I give him curses, yet he gives me love.

I am rude to him and curse him, and he responds in love.

HELENA
O that my prayers could such affection move!

I wish my prayers and well-wishing could be as powerful!

HERMIA
The more I hate, the more he follows me.

I hate him more and more, and all it does is make him follow me more.

HELENA
The more I love, the more he hateth me.

And the more I love him, the more he hates me.

HERMIA
His folly, Helena, is no fault of mine.

I have done nothing to warrant his silly feelings for me.

HELENA

None, but your beauty: would that fault were mine!

HERMIA
Take comfort: he no more shall see my face;
Lysander and myself will fly this place.
Before the time I did Lysander see,
Seem'd Athens as a paradise to me:
O, then, what graces in my love do dwell,
That he hath turn'd a heaven unto a hell!

LYSANDER
Helen, to you our minds we will unfold:
To-morrow night, when Phoebe doth behold
Her silver visage in the watery glass,
Decking with liquid pearl the bladed grass,
A time that lovers' flights doth still conceal,
Through Athens' gates have we devised to steal.

HERMIA
And in the wood, where often you and I
Upon faint primrose-beds were wont to lie,
Emptying our bosoms of their counsel sweet,
There my Lysander and myself shall meet;
And thence from Athens turn away our eyes,
To seek new friends and stranger companies.
Farewell, sweet playfellow: pray thou for us;
And good luck grant thee thy Demetrius!
Keep word, Lysander: we must starve our sight
From lovers' food till morrow deep midnight.

LYSANDER
I will, my Hermia.

Helena, adieu:
As you on him, Demetrius dote on you!

HELENA
How happy some o'er other some can be!
Through Athens I am thought as fair as she.
But what of that? Demetrius thinks not so;
He will not know what all but he do know:

No, but your beauty has done enough: I wish I had that problem.

*Don't worry, he will not see me anymore
After Lysander and I run away.
Before I met Lysander,
Athens was my paradise:
But Lysander is so wonderful
That in comparison this heaven is more like a hell!*

*Helen, we will tell you our secret:
Tomorrow night, when the moon looks down,
Like a silver eye, on a lake,
Coloring each blade of grass silver,
A time late at night that hides lovers' plans from those asleep, We have planned to leave Athens.*

*And in the forest where we used to
Lie on the flower beds
And talk about everything on our minds,
That is where Lysander and I will meet.
From then, we will no longer look at Athens
And instead seek out new friends and communities. Goodbye my friend! Pray for us
And we wish you good luck with Demetrius!
Be faithful, Lysander. Now we must not
See each otehr until late tomorrow night.*

Exit HERMIA

*Goodbye, Helena:
I hope Demetrius returns the love you give to him!*

Exit

*Some are so much happier than others!
In Athens, many think me as beautiful as Hermia, But what does that mean since Demetrius does not? He does not accept what*

And as he errs, doting on Hermia's eyes,
So I, admiring of his qualities:
Things base and vile, folding no quantity,
Love can transpose to form and dignity:
Love looks not with the eyes, but with the mind;
And therefore is wing'd Cupid painted blind:
Nor hath Love's mind of any judgement taste;
Wings and no eyes figure unheedy haste:
And therefore is Love said to be a child,
Because in choice he is so oft beguiled.
As waggish boys in game themselves forswear,
So the boy Love is perjured every where:
For ere Demetrius look'd on Hermia's eyne,
He hail'd down oaths that he was only mine;
And when this hail some heat from Hermia felt,
So he dissolved, and showers of oaths did melt.
I will go tell him of fair Hermia's flight:
Then to the wood will he to-morrow night
Pursue her; and for this intelligence
If I have thanks, it is a dear expense:
But herein mean I to enrich my pain,
To have his sight thither and back again.

*everyone else seems to agree on And while he
mistakenly obsesses over Hermia's eyes So too I
am mistaken in admiring him. Evil and
disgusting qualities Are transformed by love to
fair and noble things. Love does not look with
the same eyes others have, but with one's mind:
This is why Cupid is painted as being blind
And why Love does not have good judgement.
With wings and no eyes, Cupid is hasty
And so Love is like a child Making bad and
reckless choices. As playful boys jokingly lie,
So too does Love lie and break its promises:
Before Demetrius fell for Hermia's beauty,
He swore repeatedly to be true to me,
And then when Hermia's presence came into his
mind, He weakened his vows to me.
I will tell him of Hermia's plan
And tomorrow night he will go to the forest
And follow her. Perhaps, after telling him this,
He will be grateful, and that will make it
worthwhile, Although it will hurt me even more
To see him leave and then return again.*

Exit

Scene II

Athens. QUINCE'S house.

Enter QUINCE, SNUG, BOTTOM, FLUTE, SNOUT, and STARVELING

QUINCE
Is all our company here?

Is everyone here?

BOTTOM
You were best to call them generally, man by man,
according to the scrip.

*It would be easier to take attendance individually
by a roll-call.*

QUINCE
Here is the scroll of every man's name, which is thought fit, through all Athens, to play in our interlude before the duke and the duchess, on his wedding-day at night.

*Here is the list of the actors
that all of Athens considers talented and are
able to perform in our skit for the duke and
duchess at their wedding.*

BOTTOM
First, good Peter Quince, say what the play treats
on, then read the names of the actors, and so grow
to a point.

*Peter Quince, you should first explain what the
play is about,
and then read the cast,
for clarity's sake.*

QUINCE
Marry, our play is, The most lamentable comedy, and
most cruel death of Pyramus and Thisby.

*Of course: we will perform "The Sad Comedy
and
Cruel Death of Pyramus and Thisby."*

BOTTOM
A very good piece of work, I assure you, and a merry. Now, good Peter Quince, call forth your actors by the scroll. Masters, spread yourselves.

*A very good play, I promise, and
fun. Now, Peter Quince, call out
the actors. Everyone, spread out so you can
hear.*

QUINCE
Answer as I call you. Nick Bottom, the weaver.

*Respond when I call you. Nick Bottom, the
weaver.*

BOTTOM
Ready. Name what part I am for, and proceed.

I'm here. Who am I playing?

QUINCE
You, Nick Bottom, are set down for Pyramus.

You will play Pyramus.

BOTTOM
What is Pyramus? a lover, or a tyrant?

And who is he? A lover, a villain?

QUINCE
A lover, that kills himself most gallant for love.

A lover who nobly kills himself for love.

BOTTOM
That will ask some tears in the true performing of
it: if I do it, let the audience look to their
eyes; I will move storms, I will condole in some
measure. To the rest: yet my chief humour is for a
tyrant: I could play Ercles rarely, or a part to
tear a cat in, to make all split.
The raging rocks
And shivering shocks
Shall break the locks
Of prison gates;
And Phibbus' car
Shall shine from far
And make and mar
The foolish Fates.
This was lofty! Now name the rest of the players.
This is Ercles' vein, a tyrant's vein; a lover is
more condoling.

It sounds like I will have to cry in order to perform it well.
If so, the audience should prepare themselves:
I will cause storms and strongly emote my grief.
Now continue— but you know I play the tyrant best. I would make a good Hercules, or any part where I could yell and shout angrily, listen:

How great was that! Now continue with the other actors—
so you know, that was Hercules as a tyrant. My lover part will be much sadder.

QUINCE
Francis Flute, the bellows-mender.

Francis Flute, who repairs bellows.

FLUTE
Here, Peter Quince.

Here, Peter Quince.

QUINCE
Flute, you must take Thisby on you.

Flute, you will play Thisby.

FLUTE
What is Thisby? a wandering knight?

And who is Thisby? A knight on a quest?

QUINCE
It is the lady that Pyramus must love.

Thisby is the lady Pyramus loves.

FLUTE
Nay, faith, let me not play a woman; I have a
beard coming.

No, please, do not make me play a woman. I have a beard coming in.

QUINCE

That's all one: you shall play it in a mask, and you may speak as small as you will.

That doesn't matter – you will play it in a mask and you can make your voice high and disguised.

BOTTOM

An I may hide my face, let me play Thisby too, I'll
speak in a monstrous little voice. 'Thisne, Thisne;' 'Ah, Pyramus, lover dear! thy Thisby dear,
and lady dear!'

*If Thisby requires a mask, let me play both! I'll speak in a little voice after playing Pyramus, saying,
"Thisne! Thisne!" and then as Thisby, "Pyramus my love! I am here, your dear lady!"*

QUINCE

No, no; you must play Pyramus: and, Flute, you Thisby.

No – you will be Pyramus, and Flute will be Thisby.

BOTTOM

Well, proceed.

Fine, continue.

QUINCE

Robin Starveling, the tailor.

Robin Starveling, the tailor.

STARVELING

Here, Peter Quince.

Here, Peter Quince.

QUINCE

Robin Starveling, you must play Thisby's mother.
Tom Snout, the tinker.

Robyn, you must be Thisby's mother. Tom Snout, the repairman.

SNOUT

Here, Peter Quince.

Here, Peter Quince.

QUINCE

You, Pyramus' father: myself, Thisby's father: Snug, the joiner; you, the lion's part: and, I hope, here is a play fitted.

You are Pyramus father, and I will play Thisby's father. Snug the wood worker, you will be the lion, and I think that is everyone.

SNUG

Have you the lion's part written? pray you, if it be, give it me, for I am slow of study.

Is the lion's part finished? If so, please let me have it. It takes me a while to learn the lines.

QUINCE

You may do it extempore, for it is nothing but roaring.

You can make it all up, because it is simply roaring.

BOTTOM

Let me play the lion too: I will roar, that I will
do any man's heart good to hear me; I will roar,
that I will make the duke say 'Let him roar
again,
let him roar again.'

*Then let me play the lion as well. I will roar
so forcefully and everyone will love it,
and the duke will ask for me to roar
again and again.*

QUINCE

An you should do it too terribly, you would
fright
the duchess and the ladies, that they would
shriek;
and that were enough to hang us all.

*Then you would be too ferocious, and scare
the duchess and the women, and they would
scream.
That would be enough to hang us all.*

ALL

That would hang us, every mother's son.

They would hang every one of us!

BOTTOM

I grant you, friends, if that you should fright the
ladies out of their wits, they would have no
more
discretion but to hang us: but I will aggravate
my
voice so that I will roar you as gently as any
sucking dove; I will roar you an 'twere any
nightingale.

*Granted, if I were to scare
the women out of their minds, they would
surely hang us – but then I would change my
voice so that my roar will be as gentle
as a dove, and when I roar you will think I was
a nightingale.*

QUINCE

You can play no part but Pyramus; for Pyramus
is a
sweet-faced man; a proper man, as one shall see
in a
summer's day; a most lovely gentleman-like
man:
therefore you must needs play Pyramus.

*You will play only Pyramus since Pyramus
is a good lucking man, a noble man like one you
would
find in the summer, a handsome and chivalrous
man.
You are the only one who can be such a man.*

BOTTOM

Well, I will undertake it. What beard were I best
to play it in?

*Fine, I will do it. And how would you like my
beard to look for the part?*

QUINCE

Why, what you will.

However you want.

BOTTOM

I will discharge it in either your straw-colour
beard, your orange-tawny beard, your purple-in-

*I could wear a straw colored
beard, or an orange-red one, or a darker red*

grain
beard, or your French-crown-colour beard, your
perfect yellow.

beard, or one as yellow as the French coin
called a crown.

_____

QUINCE
Some of your French crowns have no hair at all,
and
then you will play bare-faced. But, masters, here
are your parts: and I am to entreat you, request
you and desire you, to con them by to-morrow
night;
and meet me in the palace wood, a mile without
the
town, by moonlight; there will we rehearse, for
if
we meet in the city, we shall be dogged with
company, and our devices known. In the
meantime I
will draw a bill of properties, such as our play
wants. I pray you, fail me not.

Some French kings have no hair at all,
so you would have to go without a beard.
Anyway, here
is everyone's part. I must beg and ask
you all to learn them by tomorrow night.
We will meet in the forest, about a mile
from town, and rehearse by the moonlight. If
we were to meet in the city, people would
discover us
and the play, and ruin it. In the meantime,
I will list everything we need for the play.
Please, do everything I ask.

BOTTOM
We will meet; and there we may rehearse most
obscenely and courageously. Take pains; be
perfect: adieu.

We will meet and rehearse
loudly and wonderfully. Work hard. Learn it
perfectly. Goodbye.

QUINCE
At the duke's oak we meet.

In the forest by the palace we will meet.

BOTTOM
Enough; hold or cut bow-strings.

Ok, be there or do not meet us again.

Exeunt

Act II

Scene I

A wood near Athens.

Enter, from opposite sides, a FAIRY, and PUCK

PUCK
How now, spirit! whither wander you?

Hello, spirit! Where are you going?

FAIRY
Over hill, over dale,
Thorough bush, thorough brier,
Over park, over pale,
Thorough flood, thorough fire,
I do wander everywhere,
Swifter than the moon's sphere;
And I serve the fairy queen,
To dew her orbs upon the green.
The cowslips tall her pensioners be:
In their gold coats spots you see;
Those be rubies, fairy favours,
In those freckles live their savours:
I must go seek some dewdrops here
And hang a pearl in every cowslip's ear.
Farewell, thou lob of spirits; I'll be gone:
Our queen and all our elves come here anon.

Over hill and valley
and through the bush and thorns,
over parks and gardens
and through the water and the fire.
I go everywhere
faster than it takes the moon to rise and fall
In order to serve the queen of the fairies
By watering the flowers with dew.
The cowslip flowers guard her –
Do you see the spots in their golden petals?
Those are rubies, fairy gifts,
And that is where their sweet smell comes from.
I must find some dewdrops
And hang one on each cowslip flower.
Goodbye, you bad fairy – I must leave
Since the queen and the elves will be here soon.

PUCK
The king doth keep his revels here to-night:
Take heed the queen come not within his sight;
For Oberon is passing fell and wrath,
Because that she as her attendant hath
A lovely boy, stolen from an Indian king;
She never had so sweet a changeling;
And jealous Oberon would have the child
Knight of his train, to trace the forests wild;
But she perforce withholds the loved boy,
Crowns him with flowers and makes him all her joy:
And now they never meet in grove or green,
By fountain clear, or spangled starlight sheen,
But, they do square, that all their elves for fear
Creep into acorn-cups and hide them there.

The king is having a party here tonight
So be careful to keep the queen away –
King Oberon is very angry
Since Queen Titania took a new servant,
A beautiful human boy stolen from an Indian
king. She had never stolen so sweet an orphan
And so Oberon is jealous and desires the boy
As his servant when he wanders the wild forests.
The queen refuses to give him her boy
And dotes on him, putting flowers in his hair.
Now, they never meet together in the woods
Or by a clear pond, or under the night sky,
Except to argue so fiercely that their elves
Hide in acorn shells from them.

FAIRY

Either I mistake your shape and making quite,
Or else you are that shrewd and knavish sprite
Call'd Robin Goodfellow: are not you he
That frights the maidens of the villagery;
Skim milk, and sometimes labour in the quern
And bootless make the breathless housewife churn;
And sometime make the drink to bear no barm;
Mislead night-wanderers, laughing at their harm?
Those that Hobgoblin call you and sweet Puck,
You do their work, and they shall have good luck:
Are not you he?

Either I am mistaken
Or you are that cunning prankster fairy
Named Robin Goodfellow. Isn't it you
Who scares the women in the village,
Who skims the cream off of the milk, and
sometimes increase the work Of the housewife
who is trying to churn butter
By making it stay milk?
Isn't it you who makes wanderers lost and
laughs at them?
Some call you Hobgoblin or Puck,
And whoever does gets your help, and you give
them good luck.
Isn't that you?

PUCK

Thou speak'st aright;
I am that merry wanderer of the night.
I jest to Oberon and make him smile
When I a fat and bean-fed horse beguile,
Neighing in likeness of a filly foal:
And sometime lurk I in a gossip's bowl,
In very likeness of a roasted crab,
And when she drinks, against her lips I bob
And on her wither'd dewlap pour the ale.
The wisest aunt, telling the saddest tale,
Sometime for three-foot stool mistaketh me;
Then slip I from her bum, down topples she,
And 'tailor' cries, and falls into a cough;
And then the whole quire hold their hips and laugh,
And waxen in their mirth and neeze and swear
A merrier hour was never wasted there.
But, room, fairy! here comes Oberon.

You are correct,
I am that happy traveler of the night.
I make jokes for King Oberon and make him
smile – Sometimes by tricking a calm, domestic
horse By neighing and tricking him that I am a
young filly – And sometimes I hide in an old
woman's bowl of ale Looking like a roasted
crabapple And when she drinks, I bob up to her
lips Making her spill the drink all over her
wrinkled neck. A wise aunt telling a sad story
Sometimes mistakes me for a three-foot high
stool And then when she sits, I slip from her rear
and she falls, Crying out in pain and coughing –
Then everyone laughs, holding their sides,
And have fun, and sneeze and swear:
A more joyful time was never had.
But make way, fairy! Oberon is coming.

FAIRY

And here my mistress. Would that he were gone!

And here is Queen Titania! I wish he were gone!

Enter, from one side, OBERON, with his train;
from the other, TITANIA, with hers

OBERON

Ill met by moonlight, proud Titania.

It makes me feel ill to see you, Titania.

TITANIA

What, jealous Oberon! Fairies, skip hence:

Are you jealous, Oberon? Fairies, come along:

I have forsworn his bed and company.

OBERON
Tarry, rash wanton: am not I thy lord?

TITANIA
Then I must be thy lady: but I know
When thou hast stolen away from fairy land,
And in the shape of Corin sat all day,
Playing on pipes of corn and versing love
To amorous Phillida. Why art thou here,
Come from the farthest Steppe of India?
But that, forsooth, the bouncing Amazon,
Your buskin'd mistress and your warrior love,
To Theseus must be wedded, and you come
To give their bed joy and prosperity.

OBERON
How canst thou thus for shame, Titania,
Glance at my credit with Hippolyta,
Knowing I know thy love to Theseus?
Didst thou not lead him through the glimmering night
From Perigenia, whom he ravished?
And make him with fair AEgle break his faith,
With Ariadne and Antiopa?

TITANIA
These are the forgeries of jealousy:
And never, since the middle summer's spring,
Met we on hill, in dale, forest or mead,
By paved fountain or by rushy brook,
Or in the beached margent of the sea,
To dance our ringlets to the whistling wind,
But with thy brawls thou hast disturb'd our sport.
Therefore the winds, piping to us in vain,
As in revenge, have suck'd up from the sea
Contagious fogs; which falling in the land
Have every pelting river made so proud
That they have overborne their continents:
The ox hath therefore stretch'd his yoke in vain,
The ploughman lost his sweat, and the green corn
Hath rotted ere his youth attain'd a beard;
The fold stands empty in the drowned field,

I have promised not to sleep with him or speak to him.

Stay, impulsive witch: aren't I your King, and husband?

Then I must be your Queen and wife, but I know That you snuck away from fairy-land And changed your shape to that of a shepherd, spending all day Playing music and reciting love poetry To your fling, Phillida. And why did you come here, So far from our land in India? I know why: that swaggering Amazon who was your animal skin wearing, warrior of a mistress and love, Is marrying Theseus, and you have come To celebrate and bless their union.

How can you speak so shamelessly, Titania, And attack my thoughts of Hippolyta, When you know that I know of your love for Theseus? Didn't you lead him through the night away from Perigenia, whom he raped? And didn't you make him cheat on Aegle With both Ariadne and Antiopa?

You are making this up from your jealousy. Never, since the beginning of midsummer, Can I meet with the fairies, not on a hill or in the valley, or the forest, Not by a fountain or by a stream Or on the beach next to the sea. We aren't able to dance and shake our hair in the wind Without you interrupting us to argue and fight. So, the winds, making noise in vain, Have taken their revenge by lifting up from the sea Great clouds that rain all over the land, Pelting the river until each one is puffed up, like they are proud, Spilling over their banks and flooding. The ox in the fields can't pull the yoke through the wet mud, The farmer can do nothing, and the young corn Has rotted before it grew out its yellow tassel marking its ripeness. The sheep pens are empty

And crows are fatted with the murrion flock;
The nine men's morris is fill'd up with mud,
And the quaint mazes in the wanton green
For lack of tread are undistinguishable:
The human mortals want their winter here;
No night is now with hymn or carol blest:
Therefore the moon, the governess of floods,
Pale in her anger, washes all the air,
That rheumatic diseases do abound:
And thorough this distemperature we see
The seasons alter: hoary-headed frosts
Far in the fresh lap of the crimson rose,
And on old Hiems' thin and icy crown
An odorous chaplet of sweet summer buds
Is, as in mockery, set: the spring, the summer,
The childing autumn, angry winter, change
Their wonted liveries, and the mazed world,
By their increase, now knows not which is
which:
And this same progeny of evils comes
From our debate, from our dissension;
We are their parents and original.

OBERON
Do you amend it then; it lies in you:
Why should Titania cross her Oberon?
I do but beg a little changeling boy,
To be my henchman.

TITANIA
Set your heart at rest:
The fairy land buys not the child of me.
His mother was a votaress of my order:
And, in the spiced Indian air, by night,
Full often hath she gossip'd by my side,
And sat with me on Neptune's yellow sands,
Marking the embarked traders on the flood,
When we have laugh'd to see the sails conceive
And grow big-bellied with the wanton wind;
Which she, with pretty and with swimming gait
Following,--her womb then rich with my young
squire,--
Would imitate, and sail upon the land,
To fetch me trifles, and return again,
As from a voyage, rich with merchandise.
But she, being mortal, of that boy did die;

*in the flooded fields, And crows are fat from
eating the sheep who died from disease. Places
where people could play games like "nine men's
morris" are now muddy, And mazes cut into
fields of weeds Have collapsed from the water
and are unusable. Since it is not winter for the
humans, They have not blessed the night with
their songs to protect them, And so the moon,
who controls the water, Can put water into the
air in her anger Which causes sicknesses to
arise. And since the temperatures are off for the
time of year, The seasons are changing: frosts
Are appearing on the blooming rose
And on Winter's crown of ice,
A row of sweet smelling flowers, like prayer
beads, hangs like a joke. Spring, summer, fertile
autumn, and cold, angry winter, have exchanged
their places, and now the confused world
doesn't know which season it is in.
This list of evils and poor effects all come
For our arguments and disagreement:
We are the causes.*

*Then fix it: you are the one at fault.
Why are you being mean to me?
All I want is a little orphan boy
To be my servant.*

*Let it go:
You cannot buy the child from me for all of
fairy-land. His mother worshipped me as part of
my order, And at night, in the perfumed Indian
air, She gossiped with me at my side,
And sat with me on the yellow sands of the
beach, Watching the traders in their ships out at
sea, And laughing to watch the sails grow,
Like a pregnant woman's belly, with the wind.
She, beautiful and graceful,
And already pregnant with the boy you want,
Would imitate the ships and pretend to sail on
the land,
Fetching me little gifts and returning
Like she had been on a voyage and came back
with treasures. But she was mortal, and she died*

And for her sake do I rear up her boy,
And for her sake I will not part with him.

giving birth to the boy Whom now I raise for her sake, And for her sake I will not give him to you.

OBERON
How long within this wood intend you stay?

How long are you staying in this forest?

TITANIA
Perchance till after Theseus' wedding-day.
If you will patiently dance in our round
And see our moonlight revels, go with us;
If not, shun me, and I will spare your haunts.

*Probably until after Theseus' wedding.
If you can dance with us nicely
And partake in our parties beneath the moon,
then come with us, And if not, leave me alone
and I will leave you alone.*

OBERON
Give me that boy, and I will go with thee.

Give me the boy and I will go with you.

TITANIA
Not for thy fairy kingdom. Fairies, away!
We shall chide downright, if I longer stay.

*Not for the entire kingdom. Fairies, come!
We will fight openly if I longer stay.*

Exit TITANIA with her train

OBERON
Well, go thy way: thou shalt not from this grove
Till I torment thee for this injury.
My gentle Puck, come hither. Thou rememberest
Since once I sat upon a promontory,
And heard a mermaid on a dolphin's back
Uttering such dulcet and harmonious breath
That the rude sea grew civil at her song
And certain stars shot madly from their spheres,
To hear the sea-maid's music.

*Fine, go your way. You won't leave here
Until I get my revenge for this.
Puck, come here. Do you remember
when I sat on a cliff
And heard a mermaid riding on a dolphin,
Singing such a sweet melody
That it made the stormy sea become calm
And the stars twinkled brighter
just to hear her song?*

PUCK
I remember.

OBERON
That very time I saw, but thou couldst not,
Flying between the cold moon and the earth,
Cupid all arm'd: a certain aim he took
At a fair vestal throned by the west,
And loosed his love-shaft smartly from his bow,
As it should pierce a hundred thousand hearts;
But I might see young Cupid's fiery shaft
Quench'd in the chaste beams of the watery moon,
And the imperial votaress passed on,

*Also then, I saw something you couldn't:
Flying high in the sky, between the moon and
earth, Was Cupid, armed iwth his bow. He took
aim At a vestal virgin, a worshipper sitting on a
throne in the west And shot an enchanted arrow
from his bow strongly, As if he was trying to
shoot it through a hundred thousand hearts at
once. But I saw this enflamed arrow of Cupid's
Put out by the virginal beams of the moon
And so the young royal worshipper walked on*

In maiden meditation, fancy-free.
Yet mark'd I where the bolt of Cupid fell:
It fell upon a little western flower,
Before milk-white, now purple with love's wound,
And maidens call it love-in-idleness.
Fetch me that flower; the herb I shew'd thee once:
The juice of it on sleeping eye-lids laid
Will make or man or woman madly dote
Upon the next live creature that it sees.
Fetch me this herb; and be thou here again
Ere the leviathan can swim a league.

PUCK
I'll put a girdle round about the earth
In forty minutes.

OBERON
Having once this juice,
I'll watch Titania when she is asleep,
And drop the liquor of it in her eyes.
The next thing then she waking looks upon,
Be it on lion, bear, or wolf, or bull,
On meddling monkey, or on busy ape,
She shall pursue it with the soul of love:
And ere I take this charm from off her sight,
As I can take it with another herb,
I'll make her render up her page to me.
But who comes here? I am invisible;
And I will overhear their conference.

DEMETRIUS
I love thee not, therefore pursue me not.
Where is Lysander and fair Hermia?
The one I'll slay, the other slayeth me.
Thou told'st me they were stolen unto this wood;
And here am I, and wode within this wood,
Because I cannot meet my Hermia.
Hence, get thee gone, and follow me no more.

HELENA
You draw me, you hard-hearted adamant;
But yet you draw not iron, for my heart

Meditating beautifully, and spared from the arrow. But, I saw where the arrow fell: It struck a little wester flower That had been milk white, but after turned purple where the arrow hit it. Maidens refer to it as "love-in-idleness." Bring me that flower, the one I once showed you. If its juice is put on the eyelids of someone asleep, It will make any man, woman, or creature fall in love With the next living creature it sees. Bring me this flower and return Before the great sea monster can swim a league.

I can circle the earth In forty minutes.

Exit

Once I have this flower and its potion, I will go to Titania when she is asleep And place a drop of it in her eyes. When she wakes, the next thing she sees, Whether it is a lion, bear, wolf, bull A bothersome monkey, or an ape, She will fall in love with it and pursue it. Then, before I remove this potion – Since I can do that with another flower – I will force her to give me the orphan boy. Who is coming now? Since I am invisible I will overhear their conversation.

Enter DEMETRIUS, HELENA, following him

I don't love you, now stop following me. Where are Lysander and beautiful Hermia? I will kill Lysander, while Hermia has me head over heels for her. You told me they had snuck off into this forest, And here I am, going crazy in a forest, All because I can't meet Hermia. Now go away and stop following me.

You attract me like a cruel magnet, One that must not attract iron because my heart

Is true as steel: leave you your power to draw,
And I shall have no power to follow you.

DEMETRIUS
Do I entice you? do I speak you fair?
Or, rather, do I not in plainest truth
Tell you, I do not, nor I cannot love you?

HELENA
And even for that do I love you the more.
I am your spaniel; and, Demetrius,
The more you beat me, I will fawn on you:
Use me but as your spaniel, spurn me, strike me,
Neglect me, lose me; only give me leave,
Unworthy as I am, to follow you.
What worser place can I beg in your love,--
And yet a place of high respect with me,--
Than to be used as you use your dog?

DEMETRIUS
Tempt not too much the hatred of my spirit;
For I am sick when I do look on thee.

HELENA
And I am sick when I look not on you.

DEMETRIUS
You do impeach your modesty too much,
To leave the city and commit yourself
Into the hands of one that loves you not;
To trust the opportunity of night
And the ill counsel of a desert place
With the rich worth of your virginity.

HELENA
Your virtue is my privilege: for that
It is not night when I do see your face,
Therefore I think I am not in the night;
Nor doth this wood lack worlds of company,
For you in my respect are all the world:
Then how can it be said I am alone,
When all the world is here to look on me?

DEMETRIUS
I'll run from thee and hide me in the brakes,
And leave thee to the mercy of wild beasts.

---

*Is pure, like steel. Stop pulling me to you
And I will not be forced to follow you.*

*Do I flirt with you? Do I speak kindly to you?
Or instead, am I honest with you
By saying that I do not and cannot love you?*

*Even that makes me love you more.
I am your pet dog, Demetrius:
Though you beat me, I still come to you.
Use me like a dog, turn me away, hit me,
Ignore me – just allow me,
Though I am unworthy, to follow you.
Is there any lower place in your life –
And yet I would be honored to be treated this
way – Than to be used, to be your dog?*

*Don't tempt me to be even more hateful to you.
I feel sick when I look at you.*

And I feel sick when I do not look at you.

*You are risking your reputation of modesy
By leaving the city and trusting
Someone who does not love you
And to leave yourself vulnerable at night
In the secrecy of a deserted place, far from
town, When your valuable virginity could be
taken away.*

*I know you are virtuous, and that protects me.
Anyway, your face is so bright when I look at it
That I do not think it is night time.
This forest, too, is not deserted
Because having you nearby is the same as
having the whole world. So how can you say I
am alone When the whole world is here with
me?*

*I'll run away and hide in the brush,
Leaving you to the wild animals.*

HELENA

The wildest hath not such a heart as you.
Run when you will, the story shall be changed:
Apollo flies, and Daphne holds the chase;
The dove pursues the griffin; the mild hind
Makes speed to catch the tiger; bootless speed,
When cowardice pursues and valour flies.

The wildest one is not as mean as you.
Run away then, the classic myth will be
reversed: Apollo will fly instead, and Daphne
will chase him, The dove will chase the griffin,
the deer Will run fast after the tiger, with
unmatched speed What is cowardly will chase
what is brave, which runs away.

DEMETRIUS

I will not stay thy questions; let me go:
Or, if thou follow me, do not believe
But I shall do thee mischief in the wood.

I will not listen to your questions, let me leave –
Or, if you follow me, know
That I will do evil things to you in the forest.

HELENA

Ay, in the temple, in the town, the field,
You do me mischief. Fie, Demetrius!
Your wrongs do set a scandal on my sex:
We cannot fight for love, as men may do;
We should be wood and were not made to woo.

Already in the temple and in the town and in the
field You do evil things to me! Bad Demetrius!
Your evil treatment insults women
Who cannot fight for love like men do,
Instead we should be the ones courted, not the
courters.

Exit DEMETRIUS

I'll follow thee and make a heaven of hell,
To die upon the hand I love so well.

I'll follow you and the evil you give will be
heaven and joy to me, Even joy to be killed by
someone I love so much.

Exit

OBERON

Fare thee well, nymph: ere he do leave this grove,
Thou shalt fly him and he shall seek thy love.

Good luck, young girl. Before Demetrius leaves
the forest, You will be running from him, and he
will be chasing you.

Re-enter PUCK

Hast thou the flower there? Welcome, wanderer.

Do you have the flower? Hello, wandering
Puck.

PUCK

Ay, there it is.

Yes, here it is.

OBERON

I pray thee, give it me.
I know a bank where the wild thyme blows,
Where oxlips and the nodding violet grows,
Quite over-canopied with luscious woodbine,
With sweet musk-roses and with eglantine:

Please, give it to me.
There is a bank I know where wild thyme
And oxlip and violet flowers grow,
Shaded by overgrowths of honeysuckle
And musk-roses and sweet briars:

There sleeps Titania sometime of the night,
Lull'd in these flowers with dances and delight;
And there the snake throws her enamell'd skin,
Weed wide enough to wrap a fairy in:
And with the juice of this I'll streak her eyes,
And make her full of hateful fantasies.
Take thou some of it, and seek through this grove:
A sweet Athenian lady is in love
With a disdainful youth: anoint his eyes;
But do it when the next thing he espies
May be the lady: thou shalt know the man
By the Athenian garments he hath on.
Effect it with some care, that he may prove
More fond on her than she upon her love:
And look thou meet me ere the first cock crow.

PUCK
Fear not, my lord, your servant shall do so.

Sometimes Titania sleeps there at night Attracted to the flowers after her dancing and frolicking. There, the snake covers her in a blanket of its shed skin And the fairies wrap themselves in the wide weeds, It is there that I will place this potion on her eyes And make her fall madly in love. Now you take some of it as well, and look for
A sweet Athenian lady who is in love With a young man who does not love her. Put this on his eyes, But do it so that the next thing he sees Is the woman. You will know the man By his Athenian clothing.
Make sure you apply the potion so that he Will love her more than she loves him, And then meet me before the first crowing of the rooster.

Don't worry, my king, I will do everything you ask.

Exeunt

28

Scene II

Another part of the wood.

Enter TITANIA, with her train

TITANIA
Come, now a roundel and a fairy song;
Then, for the third part of a minute, hence;
Some to kill cankers in the musk-rose buds,
Some war with rere-mice for their leathern
wings,
To make my small elves coats, and some keep
back
The clamorous owl that nightly hoots and
wonders
At our quaint spirits. Sing me now asleep;
Then to your offices and let me rest.

Come and we will dance and sing,
And then, for a little while after,
Some of you will kill worms infecting the flowers
And some fight the bats to take their leathery
wings
So I can make coats from them for small elves,
and some of you
Will chase off that noisy owl that hoots every
night
At our festivities. Now, sing me to sleep,
And then go to work and let me rest.

The Fairies sing

FIRST FAIRY
You spotted snakes with double tongue,
Thorny hedgehogs, be not seen;
Newts and blind-worms, do no wrong,
Come not near our fairy queen.

You forked tongue snakes
And porcupines, go away;
Newts and lizards, do not do anything wrong,
And stay away from Queen Titania.

FAIRIES
Philomel, with melody
Sing in our sweet lullaby;
Lulla, lulla, lullaby, lulla, lulla, lullaby:
Never harm,
Nor spell nor charm,
Come our lovely lady nigh;
So, good night, with lullaby.

Dear nightingale, melodiously
Sing with us in this lullaby.

Let no harm
Or spell or enchantment
Come to our lovely queen here.
Now goodnight, and sweet dreams.

FIRST FAIRY
Weaving spiders, come not here;
Hence, you long-legg'd spinners, hence!
Beetles black, approach not near;
Worm nor snail, do no offence.

Spiders weaving your webs, stay away,
All of you long-legged spinners of webs, stay
back! Black beetles, do not come near,
And worm and snail, do nothing wrong.

FAIRIES
Philomel, with melody
Sing in our sweet lullaby;
Lulla, lulla, lullaby, lulla, lulla, lullaby:
Never harm,

Dear nightingale, melodiously
Sing with us in this lullaby.

Let no harm

Nor spell nor charm,
Come our lovely lady nigh;
So, good night, with lullaby.

FAIRY
Hence, away! now all is well:
One aloof stand sentinel.

Or spell or enchantment
Come to our lovely queen here.
Now goodnight, and sweet dreams.

Stop, and let us go! Everything is well.
One of you stay here to guard.

Exeunt Fairies. TITANIA sleeps

Enter OBERON and squeezes the flower on
TITANIA's eyelids

OBERON
What thou seest when thou dost wake,
Do it for thy true-love take,
Love and languish for his sake:
Be it ounce, or cat, or bear,
Pard, or boar with bristled hair,
In thy eye that shall appear
When thou wakest, it is thy dear:
Wake when some vile thing is near.

Whatever you see when you wake up
You will believe is your true love.
Love, and feel the pain of love for the sake of the
orphan boy, Whether it is a snow leopard, or a
cat, or a bear Or a leopard, or a bristled boar —
In your eye it will appear,
When you wake, as your beloved: So I hope you
wake when something nasty is near.

Exit

Enter LYSANDER and HERMIA

LYSANDER
Fair love, you faint with wandering in the wood;
And to speak troth, I have forgot our way:
We'll rest us, Hermia, if you think it good,
And tarry for the comfort of the day.

My love, you look weak from walking so much in
this forest, And to tell the truth, I have gotten
lost. We should rest now, Hermia, if you think
that's a good idea, And wait for daylight.

HERMIA
Be it so, Lysander: find you out a bed;
For I upon this bank will rest my head.

I agree with you, Lysander: find yourself a bed,
because I will rest against this bank.

LYSANDER
One turf shall serve as pillow for us both;
One heart, one bed, two bosoms and one troth.

It will be a pillow for both of us,
One pillow, for one bed, for one heart shared by
two people with one truth.

HERMIA
Nay, good Lysander; for my sake, my dear,
Lie further off yet, do not lie so near.
O, take the sense, sweet, of my innocence!
Love takes the meaning in love's conference.
I mean, that my heart unto yours is knit

No, good Lysander, please, my love,
Find a place farther away, do not sleep so close
to me. Oh my dear, please recognize my good
intentions! Those in love should understand
each other. What I mean is that my heart is tied

So that but one heart we can make of it;
Two bosoms interchained with an oath;
So then two bosoms and a single troth.
Then by your side no bed-room me deny;
For lying so, Hermia, I do not lie.

HERMIA
Lysander riddles very prettily:
Now much beshrew my manners and my pride,
If Hermia meant to say Lysander lied.
But, gentle friend, for love and courtesy
Lie further off; in human modesty,
Such separation as may well be said
Becomes a virtuous bachelor and a maid,
So far be distant; and, good night, sweet friend:
Thy love ne'er alter till thy sweet life end!

LYSANDER
Amen, amen, to that fair prayer, say I;
And then end life when I end loyalty!
Here is my bed: sleep give thee all his rest!

HERMIA
With half that wish the wisher's eyes be press'd!

PUCK
Through the forest have I gone.
But Athenian found I none,
On whose eyes I might approve
This flower's force in stirring love.
Night and silence.--Who is here?
Weeds of Athens he doth wear:
This is he, my master said,
Despised the Athenian maid;
And here the maiden, sleeping sound,
On the dank and dirty ground.
Pretty soul! she durst not lie
Near this lack-love, this kill-courtesy.
Churl, upon thy eyes I throw
All the power this charm doth owe.
When thou wakest, let love forbid
Sleep his seat on thy eyelid:
So awake when I am gone;

to yours So that we have, in essence, one heart:
Two people bound with a single oath,
Two people who share one truth.
So do not deny me space to sleep beside you–
By lying there, I will not lie to your honor and
disrespect you.

Lysander speaks very nicely:
I would betray my manners and honor
If I were to imply that Lysander was a liar.
But, my friend, for love and politeness,
Lie farther away. It is modest
For such separation to be between
A virtuous bachelor and a virtuous maid,
So be distant. And now, goodnight sweet friend:
I hope your love never changes until your dear
life ends!

I say amen to that prayer,
And I hope my life ends if I should be disloyal to
you! I will sleep over here, sleep well and be
rested!

You too, Lysander, sleep well also!

They sleep.

Enter PUCK

I have gone through the entire forest
But have not found the Athenian
Whose eyes I must drug
With this flower's potion to enchant him.
Only night and silence – but who is this?
He wears Athenian clothing:
It must be him, the one my master told me about,
Who turned away the Athenian girl.
And here is the girl, sound asleep
On the wet and dirty ground.
Pretty girl! She should not lie
Near this cold and rude man.
Scoundrel, I put on your eyes
The full force of this potion.
I hope, when you wake up, that love keeps
Your eyes open.
Now wake after I leave–

For I must now to Oberon.

I must return to King Oberon.

Exit

Enter DEMETRIUS and HELENA, running

HELENA
Stay, though thou kill me, sweet Demetrius.

Wait, Demetrius, even if you kill me!

DEMETRIUS
I charge thee, hence, and do not haunt me thus.

I beg you, leave and do not keep following me.

HELENA
O, wilt thou darkling leave me? do not so.

Oh please do not leave me alone in the dark!

DEMETRIUS
Stay, on thy peril: I alone will go.

Stay at your own risk then – I can continue alone.

Exit

HELENA
O, I am out of breath in this fond chase!
The more my prayer, the lesser is my grace.
Happy is Hermia, wheresoe'er she lies;
For she hath blessed and attractive eyes.
How came her eyes so bright? Not with salt tears:
If so, my eyes are oftener wash'd than hers.
No, no, I am as ugly as a bear;
For beasts that meet me run away for fear:
Therefore no marvel though Demetrius
Do, as a monster fly my presence thus.
What wicked and dissembling glass of mine
Made me compare with Hermia's sphery eyne?
But who is here? Lysander! on the ground!
Dead? or asleep? I see no blood, no wound.
Lysander if you live, good sir, awake.

I am out of breath from chasing after Demetrius! The more I pray for him, the less I receive in return. Hermia is blessed, wherever she is, For she has beautiful eyes.
How did her eyes become this beautiful? Not from the salt of tears: If so, my eyes are washed from tears more often and would be prettier.
No, instead I am as ugly as a bear,
Even animals that see me run away, scared.
Therefore it's no surprise that Demetrius
Flees, as even a monster would run away from my looks. What evil and deceiving mirror Made me think I could compare to Hermia's beauty? Who is this? Lysander! On the ground! Is he dead or asleep? I don't see a wound or any blood. Lysander, if you are alive, wake up!

LYSANDER
[Awaking] And run through fire I will for thy sweet sake.
Transparent Helena! Nature shows art,
That through thy bosom makes me see thy heart.
Where is Demetrius? O, how fit a word
Is that vile name to perish on my sword!

And I will then run through fire for you.
Beautiful Helena! Nature has skillfully Made me able to see through your chest and right into your heart.
Where is Demetrius? Oh the one who belongs To that name will die on my sword!

HELENA

Do not say so, Lysander; say not so
What though he love your Hermia? Lord, what though?
Yet Hermia still loves you: then be content.

Don't say that, Lysander. Who
Cares if he loves Hermia? Who cares?
Hermia loves you instead, so be at peace.

LYSANDER

Content with Hermia! No; I do repent
The tedious minutes I with her have spent.
Not Hermia but Helena I love:
Who will not change a raven for a dove?
The will of man is by his reason sway'd;
And reason says you are the worthier maid.
Things growing are not ripe until their season
So I, being young, till now ripe not to reason;
And touching now the point of human skill,
Reason becomes the marshal to my will
And leads me to your eyes, where I o'erlook
Love's stories written in love's richest book.

At peace with Hermia! No, I regret
Spending these painful minutes with her.
I love Helena, not Hermia:
Who would not trade a raven for a pure dove?
A man's reason guides his will
And my reason says you are much worthier than
Hermia. Plants do not get ripe until they are old
enough, And the same is true for me: I was not
ripe enough to see you until now. Now, as to
human abilities: Reason has changed my desires
And lead them to your eyes, in which I see
The greatest stories of love in love's best book.

HELENA

Wherefore was I to this keen mockery born?
When at your hands did I deserve this scorn?
Is't not enough, is't not enough, young man,
That I did never, no, nor never can,
Deserve a sweet look from Demetrius' eye,
But you must flout my insufficiency?
Good troth, you do me wrong, good sooth, you do,
In such disdainful manner me to woo.
But fare you well: perforce I must confess
I thought you lord of more true gentleness.
O, that a lady, of one man refused.
Should of another therefore be abused!

Why was I born to be made fun of?
When have I deserved to be treated so rudely by
you? Isn't it more than enough, young man,
That I have never, and will never,
Receive a kind look from Demetrius?
And on top of that now you mock my
shortcomings to Hermia?
Seriously, you are treating me evilly
By speaking to me so disdainfully.
Now, goodbye. Though first I must say
That I thought you were much more noble.
I am already a lady one man refuses,
And now must I be one that another treats
poorly?

Exit

LYSANDER

She sees not Hermia. Hermia, sleep thou there:
And never mayst thou come Lysander near!
For as a surfeit of the sweetest things
The deepest loathing to the stomach brings,
Or as tie heresies that men do leave
Are hated most of those they did deceive,
So thou, my surfeit and my heresy,
Of all be hated, but the most of me!
And, all my powers, address your love and

She didn't see Hermia. Hermia, stay asleep
And never come near me again!
I feel overstuffed with sweet things, like how
eating desserts Makes the stomach feel ill.
Or, false beliefs that men stop believing
Are hated most by the men they formerly
deceived. So you, Hermia, whom I have been
overstuffed with, and whom I falsely believed in,
You will be hated most by me!

might
To honour Helen and to be her knight!

HERMIA
[Awaking] Help me, Lysander, help me! do thy best
To pluck this crawling serpent from my breast!
Ay me, for pity! what a dream was here!
Lysander, look how I do quake with fear:
Methought a serpent eat my heart away,
And you sat smiling at his cruel pray.
Lysander! what, removed? Lysander! lord!
What, out of hearing? gone? no sound, no word?
Alack, where are you speak, an if you hear;
Speak, of all loves! I swoon almost with fear.
No? then I well perceive you all not nigh
Either death or you I'll find immediately.

I will turn all of my power and strength and love
Toward Helen in order to win her!

Exit

Lysander, help me! Do something
And get this snake off of me!
Oh my! What a dream that was!
Lysander, look how much I am shivering from fright:
I thought a serpent was eating my heart
While you sat by smiling and watching.
Lysander! What, is he gone? Lysander!
Can he not hear me? Is he gone without giving me notice? If you hear me speak,
Speak, Lysander! I am almost fainting from fear.
No? Then I suppose you are not nearby.
I will either die, or find you right away.

Exit

Act III

Scene I

The wood. TITANIA lying asleep.

Enter QUINCE, SNUG, BOTTOM, FLUTE, SNOUT, and STARVELING

BOTTOM
Are we all met?

Is everyone here?

QUINCE
Pat, pat; and here's a marvellous convenient place
for our rehearsal. This green plot shall be our
stage, this hawthorn-brake our tiring-house; and we
will do it in action as we will do it before the duke.

Everyone is on time even. This is a perfect place to rehearse the play. The green area over there will be the stage and this large bush our dressing room. We will perform it exactly as we will in front of the duke.

BOTTOM
Peter Quince,--

Peter Quince--

QUINCE
What sayest thou, bully Bottom?

What is it, good Bottom?

BOTTOM
There are things in this comedy of Pyramus and
Thisby that will never please. First, Pyramus must
draw a sword to kill himself; which the ladies
cannot abide. How answer you that?

I am worried that some parts of this comedy of Pyramus and Thisby will not be acceptable. For example, Pyramus kills himself with a sword, something ladies cannot watch. What can we do about that?

SNOUT
By'r lakin, a parlous fear.

By God, that's a scary problem.

STARVELING
I believe we must leave the killing out, when all is done.

It seems we must leave out the suicide.

BOTTOM
Not a whit: I have a device to make all well.
Write me a prologue; and let the prologue seem to
say, we will do no harm with our swords, and

No, we won't: I have an idea to make it work well. Write a prologue that I can say before the play starts, saying that we will not hurt anyone with our swords,

35

that
Pyramus is not killed indeed; and, for the more
better assurance, tell them that I, Pyramus, am
not
Pyramus, but Bottom the weaver: this will put
them
out of fear.

and that
Pyramus does not actually die – actually, even
better, tell them that I am not really
Pyramus, but am Bottom the weaver. Saying this
will
calm their fears.

QUINCE
Well, we will have such a prologue; and it shall
be
written in eight and six.

Okay, and we will write that prologue in
ballad form.

BOTTOM
No, make it two more; let it be written in eight
and eight.

No, make each line even syllables.

SNOUT
Will not the ladies be afeard of the lion?

Won't the ladies be afraid of the lion?

STARVELING
I fear it, I promise you.

I am worried about that, really.

BOTTOM
Masters, you ought to consider with yourselves:
to
bring in--God shield us!--a lion among ladies, is
a
most dreadful thing; for there is not a more
fearful
wild-fowl than your lion living; and we ought to
look to 't.

Yes, friends, we should all think about this: to
bring a lion – a lion! – into the company of
women, is an
awful thing. There is not a scarier
bird alive than a lion, and we would do well
to think about this.

SNOUT
Therefore another prologue must tell he is not a
lion.

So why not write another prologue explaining
that he is not a real lion?

BOTTOM
Nay, you must name his name, and half his face
must
be seen through the lion's neck: and he himself
must speak through, saying thus, or to the same
defect,--'Ladies,'--or 'Fair-ladies--I would wish
You,'--or 'I would request you,'--or 'I would
entreat you,--not to fear, not to tremble: my life
for yours. If you think I come hither as a lion, it

That's not enough: we must name the actor, and
show half the face
through the lion's neck. And he should
speak directly to the audience, saying something
like, "Ladies," or "Fair ladies, I hope"
or, "I would like to ask you," or "I
beg of you, do not be afraid. I am as concerned
for your life as I am mine. If you think I am

were pity of my life: no I am no such thing; I am a
man as other men are;' and there indeed let him name
his name, and tell them plainly he is Snug the joiner.

*actually a lion, I would be ashamed: I am not, I am only
a man like these other men." And then make him
say plainly that he is Snug the joiner.*

QUINCE
Well it shall be so. But there is two hard things;
that is, to bring the moonlight into a chamber; for,
you know, Pyramus and Thisby meet by moonlight.

*Alright, that is all fine. Now there are two
difficulties. One is how to get the moonlight into
the room, since
as you all know, Pyramus and Thisby meet
beneath the moon.*

SNOUT
Doth the moon shine that night we play our play?

*Is there a full moon or a bright moon the night
we are to perform?*

BOTTOM
A calendar, a calendar! look in the almanac; find
out moonshine, find out moonshine.

*Someone get a calendar or an almanac and find
out how the moon is shining that night.*

QUINCE
Yes, it doth shine that night.

Yes, it is bright that night.

BOTTOM
Why, then may you leave a casement of the great
chamber window, where we play, open, and the moon
may shine in at the casement.

*Well then all we have to do is leave open
the big window in the room where we play, and
the moon
will shine into the room.*

QUINCE
Ay; or else one must come in with a bush of thorns
and a lanthorn, and say he comes to disfigure, or to
present, the person of Moonshine. Then, there is
another thing: we must have a wall in the great
chamber; for Pyramus and Thisby says the story, did
talk through the chink of a wall.

*Yes, that or someone could come in with a
thornbush
and a lantern and explain that he is the
representation
of the character of Moonshine. Also, there is
another difficulty: we need a wall to put in the
chamber room, since Pyramus and Thisby in the
story
talk to each other through a hole in the wall.*

SNOUT
You can never bring in a wall. What say you, Bottom?

*We cannot bring in a wall. What do you think,
Bottom?*

BOTTOM

Some man or other must present Wall: and let him
have some plaster, or some loam, or some rough-cast
about him, to signify wall; and let him hold his
fingers thus, and through that cranny shall Pyramus
and Thisby whisper.

Someone needs to play the Wall, then – we can give him
some plaster or some clay or some gravel to put on him so he looks like a wall, and he can hold his fingers like this, and through that hole Pyramus
and Thisby can whisper.

QUINCE

If that may be, then all is well. Come, sit down,
every mother's son, and rehearse your parts.
Pyramus, you begin: when you have spoken your
speech, enter into that brake: and so every one
according to his cue.

If we can do that, then we are in good shape.
Come and sit, everyone, and rehearse your parts. Pyramus, you first: after you have finished your
speech go behind the bush, and everyone else, do the same thing
when it is your cue to exit the stage.

Enter PUCK behind

PUCK

What hempen home-spuns have we swaggering here,
So near the cradle of the fairy queen?
What, a play toward! I'll be an auditor;
An actor too, perhaps, if I see cause.

Who are these poorly clothed hicks prancing about
So close to where the queen sleep?
Oh so this is a play! I will be an audience member then, And perhaps an actor too, if I want.

QUINCE

Speak, Pyramus. Thisby, stand forth.

Speak now, Pyramus; Thisby, be ready.

BOTTOM

Thisby, the flowers of odious savours sweet,--

Thisby, these flowers of sweet, odious tastes--

QUINCE

Odours, odours.

Odors, not odious.

BOTTOM

--odours savours sweet:
So hath thy breath, my dearest Thisby dear.
But hark, a voice! stay thou but here awhile,
And by and by I will to thee appear.

--odors tastes sweet:
So does your breath, my dear Thisby.
But listen, a voice! Wait here for a little
And soon enough I will come back.

Exit

PUCK

A stranger Pyramus than e'er played here.

I have never seen a stranger Pyramus.

FLUTE
Must I speak now?

Do I go now?

Exit

QUINCE
Ay, marry, must you; for you must understand he goes
but to see a noise that he heard, and is to come again.

Yes, of course, now you speak. Know that at this point, he leaves
to check on a noise that he heard, and will then come back.

FLUTE
Most radiant Pyramus, most lily-white of hue,
Of colour like the red rose on triumphant brier,
Most brisky juvenal and eke most lovely Jew,
As true as truest horse that yet would never tire,
I'll meet thee, Pyramus, at Ninny's tomb.

Most beautiful Pyramus, as white as a lily,
As red as the rose on the rosebush,
An energetic young man and a handsome Jew,
As dependable as the best horse that never gets tired, I'll meet you, Pyramus, at Ninny's tomb.

QUINCE
'Ninus' tomb,' man: why, you must not speak that
yet; that you answer to Pyramus: you speak all your
part at once, cues and all Pyramus enter: your cue
is past; it is, 'never tire.'

That's "Ninus' tomb," Flute, and you aren't supposed to say that
yet. That's your response to Pyramus: first you say
your part, and after Pyramus enters again, your cue
passes at "never tire," that is your last line before Pyramus speaks again.

FLUTE
O,--As true as truest horse, that yet would never tire.

I see -- As dependable as the best horse that never gets tired,

Re-enter PUCK, and BOTTOM with an ass's head

BOTTOM
If I were fair, Thisby, I were only thine.

If I were the most handsome man, Thisbuy, you would still be my one and only.

QUINCE
O monstrous! O strange! we are haunted. Pray, masters! fly, masters! Help!

How awful! How strange! We are being haunted! Everyone, pray and run away! Help!

Exeunt QUINCE, SNUG, FLUTE, SNOUT, and STARVELING

PUCK
I'll follow you, I'll lead you about a round,
Through bog, through bush, through brake, through brier:
Sometime a horse I'll be, sometime a hound,

I'll follow you and lead you in a circle,
Through bogs and bushes, through thickets and thorns:
Sometimes I'll be a horse, and sometimes a dog,

A hog, a headless bear, sometime a fire;
And neigh, and bark, and grunt, and roar, and
burn,
Like horse, hound, hog, bear, fire, at every turn.

BOTTOM
Why do they run away? this is a knavery of
them to
make me afeard.

SNOUT
O Bottom, thou art changed! what do I see on
thee?

BOTTOM
What do you see? you see an asshead of your
own, do
you?

QUINCE
Bless thee, Bottom! bless thee! thou art
translated.

BOTTOM
I see their knavery: this is to make an ass of me;
to fright me, if they could. But I will not stir
from this place, do what they can: I will walk up
and down here, and I will sing, that they shall
hear
I am not afraid.

The ousel cock so black of hue,
With orange-tawny bill,
The throstle with his note so true,
The wren with little quill,--

TITANIA
[Awaking] What angel wakes me from my
flowery bed?

*Sometimes a pig, or a headless bear, or a fire,
And I will neigh, bark, grunt, roar and burn,
Like each of those things to scare you common-
folk.*

Exit

*Why are they running away? This is some mean
joke
they are doing to scare me.*

Re-enter SNOUT

*Bottom, you have been turned into something
else! What is this on your neck?*

*What are you talking about? You are acting like
an ass.*

Exit SNOUT

Re-enter QUINCE

*God bless you, Bottom! You have been
changed into something else!*

Exit

*I see right through their joke. They are trying to
make me a fool and frighten me, but I will not
leave here, no matter what they do to me. I will
walk all around, and I will sing, and they will
hear me and know
that I am not afraid.
Sings
The blackbird, feathers so black,
With a dark brown bill,
The thrush with his pure song
And the wren with its small feathers--*

*Who is this waking me from my bed of flowers
with the voice of an angel?*

BOTTOM

[Sings]
The finch, the sparrow and the lark,
The plain-song cuckoo gray,
Whose note full many a man doth mark,
And dares not answer nay;--
for, indeed, who would set his wit to so foolish
a bird? who would give a bird the lie, though he
cry
'cuckoo' never so?

The finch, the sparrow, and the lark,
The gray cuckoo who sings a plain song,
Whose words many men hear
And do not dare to say no to --
Because really, who would be rash enough to
set himself agains such a silly bird? Who would
so completely doubt the bird and think his cry
that points out the cuckold is wrong?

TITANIA

I pray thee, gentle mortal, sing again:
Mine ear is much enamour'd of thy note;
So is mine eye enthralled to thy shape;
And thy fair virtue's force perforce doth move
me
On the first view to say, to swear, I love thee.

Please, mortal human, sing again;
I love to hear your beautiful voice,
And I love to look on your handsome shape.
All of your good qualities move me
On first sight and they make me swear that I
love you.

BOTTOM

Methinks, mistress, you should have little reason
for that: and yet, to say the truth, reason and
love keep little company together now-a-days;
the
more the pity that some honest neighbours will
not
make them friends. Nay, I can gleek upon
occasion.

Lady, I think you have very little reason
for that. But on the other hand, truth, reason,
and
love do not often go together...
it's too bad some mutual neighbors do not
introduce them to each other. Oh but I am only
joking.

TITANIA

Thou art as wise as thou art beautiful.

You are as wise as you are beautiful.

BOTTOM

Not so, neither: but if I had wit enough to get
out
of this wood, I have enough to serve mine own
turn.

I am not that either. But if I had enough brains
to get out
of this forest, I would have enough for my life.

TITANIA

Out of this wood do not desire to go:
Thou shalt remain here, whether thou wilt or no.
I am a spirit of no common rate;
The summer still doth tend upon my state;
And I do love thee: therefore, go with me;
I'll give thee fairies to attend on thee,
And they shall fetch thee jewels from the deep,

Do not wish to leave this forest:
You will stay here, whether you want to or not.
I am not some common spirit –
Even the summer does what I want it to –
And I love you, so you will come with me.
I will give you fairies to be your servants
And they will get you jewels from the ocean

And sing while thou on pressed flowers dost sleep;
And I will purge thy mortal grossness so
That thou shalt like an airy spirit go.
Peaseblossom! Cobweb! Moth! and Mustardseed!

And sing while you sleep on the flowers.
I will purge your mortal humanness
Until you are a spirit like me.
Peaseblossom, Cobweb, Moth, and
Mustardseed!

Enter PEASEBLOSSOM, COBWEB, MOTH, and MUSTARDSEED
PEASEBLOSSOM

Ready.

I'm ready.

COBWEB
And I.

Me too.

MOTH
And I.

Me too.

MUSTARDSEED
And I.

And me.

ALL
Where shall we go?

Where should we go?

TITANIA
Be kind and courteous to this gentleman;
Hop in his walks and gambol in his eyes;
Feed him with apricocks and dewberries,
With purple grapes, green figs, and mulberries;
The honey-bags steal from the humble-bees,
And for night-tapers crop their waxen thighs
And light them at the fiery glow-worm's eyes,
To have my love to bed and to arise;
And pluck the wings from Painted butterflies
To fan the moonbeams from his sleeping eyes:
Nod to him, elves, and do him courtesies.

Treat this man kindly and politely.
Jump and dance in front of him,
Feed him apricots and blackberries,
And grapes, figs, and mulberries.
Steal honey from the bumblebees for him
And make candles from their wax
Which you can light with the glowworm's eyes,
So my love will have light when he goes to bed
and wakes up. Pluck the wings of butterflies
And use them to keep the bright moonbeams
from his eyes when he is asleep. Bow to him, my
fairy elves, and do what he wishes.

PEASEBLOSSOM
Hail, mortal!

Hello, human!

COBWEB
Hail!

Hello!

MOTH
Hail!

Hello!

MUSTARDSEED
Hail!

Hello!

BOTTOM
I cry your worships' mercy, heartily: I beseech your
worship's name.

Please, you fairies, tell me, what are your names?

COBWEB
Cobweb.

Cobweb.

BOTTOM
I shall desire you of more acquaintance, good Master
Cobweb: if I cut my finger, I shall make bold with
you. Your name, honest gentleman?

I hope to get to know you better, Master Cobweb. If I cut my finger, I can use you to bandage the wound.
And what is your name?

PEASEBLOSSOM
Peaseblossom.

Peaseblossom.

BOTTOM
I pray you, commend me to Mistress Squash, your
mother, and to Master Peascod, your father. Good
Master Peaseblossom, I shall desire you of more
acquaintance too. Your name, I beseech you, sir?

Do give my regards to your mother Mistress Squash
and your father, Master Peascod. I hope to know you better as well Master Peaseblossom.
And your name?

MUSTARDSEED
Mustardseed.

Mustardseed.

BOTTOM
Good Master Mustardseed, I know your patience well:
that same cowardly, giant-like ox-beef hath devoured many a gentleman of your house: I promise
you your kindred had made my eyes water ere now. I
desire your more acquaintance, good Master Mustardseed.

Master Mustardseed, I know how patient you are:
cuts of cow and ox have ended many of your relatives' lives because of their use as a condiment on the meat. And to me, your relatives have made my eyes water from their pungent scent. I hope to know you better, good Master Mustardseed.

TITANIA
Come, wait upon him; lead him to my bower.

Come and wait on him, and lead him to my

The moon methinks looks with a watery eye;
And when she weeps, weeps every little flower,
Lamenting some enforced chastity.
Tie up my love's tongue bring him silently.

room. I think the moon looks like it does when the sky is about to rain: And when the moon rains, every little flower does as well, Both grieving from being forced to abstain from sex. Keep my love quiet, and bring him quietly.

Exeunt

Scene II

Another part of the wood.

Enter OBERON

OBERON

I wonder if Titania be awaked;
Then, what it was that next came in her eye,
Which she must dote on in extremity.

I wonder if Titania has awoken yet.
And then I wonder what came into her vision,
What it is she is forced to love so extremely.

Enter PUCK

Here comes my messenger.
How now, mad spirit!
What night-rule now about this haunted grove?

Here comes my messanger.
How are things, crazy spirit?
What trouble have you created in this haunted forest?

PUCK

My mistress with a monster is in love.
Near to her close and consecrated bower,
While she was in her dull and sleeping hour,
A crew of patches, rude mechanicals,
That work for bread upon Athenian stalls,
Were met together to rehearse a play
Intended for great Theseus' nuptial-day.
The shallowest thick-skin of that barren sort,
Who Pyramus presented, in their sport
Forsook his scene and enter'd in a brake
When I did him at this advantage take,
An ass's nole I fixed on his head:
Anon his Thisbe must be answered,
And forth my mimic comes. When they him spy,
As wild geese that the creeping fowler eye,
Or russet-pated choughs, many in sort,
Rising and cawing at the gun's report,
Sever themselves and madly sweep the sky,
So, at his sight, away his fellows fly;
And, at our stamp, here o'er and o'er one falls;
He murder cries and help from Athens calls.
Their sense thus weak, lost with their fears thus strong,
Made senseless things begin to do them wrong;
For briers and thorns at their apparel snatch;
Some sleeves, some hats, from yielders all things catch.

Queen Titania is in love with a monster.
Near to where she sleeps,
And while she was still fast asleep,
A collective of commoners
That work for each day's bread in Athens,
Met together to rehearse a play
They intend to perform for Theseus' wedding.
The dumbest of that ugly group,
Who play Pyramus,
Left after his scene and went behind some bushes Which is where I took advantage of him By changing his head into that of a donkey.
Soon enough, Thisby called him out
And he came forth, donkey head and all. When the group saw him,
Like wild geese that see the hunter,
Or spotted crows in a group,
Rising from the ground and cawing at the sound of a gun, Break from the group and fly quickly away, So to, at sight of him, his friends ran away. And of course here one falls again and again, While another cries out "Murder!" and seeks help from Athens. With their senses now weakened from their strong fear,
They made whatever was around them hurt them: Thorns and briars caught at their clothes, And sleeves and hats.
I led them away, scared like this,

I led them on in this distracted fear,
And left sweet Pyramus translated there:
When in that moment, so it came to pass,
Titania waked and straightway loved an ass.

And left Pyramus standing there, his head a donkey's,
When right at that moment, incredibly,
Titania woke up and began to love this donkey-man.

OBERON
This falls out better than I could devise.
But hast thou yet latch'd the Athenian's eyes
With the love-juice, as I did bid thee do?

This is better than I could have planned myself.
And did you put the potion on the Athenian's eyes Like I asked you to?

PUCK
I took him sleeping,--that is finish'd too,--
And the Athenian woman by his side:
That, when he waked, of force she must be eyed.

I found him already asleep and finished that as well, The Athenian woman sleeping next to him.
So when he wakes, she will be the one he sees.

Enter HERMIA and DEMETRIUS

OBERON
Stand close: this is the same Athenian.

Stay here, this is the same Athenian I saw earlier.

PUCK
This is the woman, but not this the man.

This is the same woman... but this is not the man I saw.

DEMETRIUS
O, why rebuke you him that loves you so?
Lay breath so bitter on your bitter foe.

Oh why do you scold the man who loves you so much? Save your cruel words for a cruel enemy.

HERMIA
Now I but chide; but I should use thee worse,
For thou, I fear, hast given me cause to curse,
If thou hast slain Lysander in his sleep,
Being o'er shoes in blood, plunge in the deep,
And kill me too.
The sun was not so true unto the day
As he to me: would he have stolen away
From sleeping Hermia? I'll believe as soon
This whole earth may be bored and that the moon
May through the centre creep and so displease
Her brother's noontide with Antipodes.
It cannot be but thou hast murder'd him;
So should a murderer look, so dead, so grim.

This is nothing, but I should be treating you worse Because I'm afraid you have given me reason to curse you. If you have killed Lysander while he was asleep, Then, since you are already walking in blood, continue on And kill me too. The sun didn't shine on the day as steadily As he loved me: why would he have left Me while sleeping? I will believe that he did that as soon As the earth gets a hole drilled through it and the moon
Passes through the hole, disturbing
The tides at noon with its pull from a place opposite where it usually is. The only answer is that you murdered him; You look like a murderer anyway, so pale and ugly.

DEMETRIUS
So should the murder'd look, and so should I,
Pierced through the heart with your stern cruelty:

A murdered person looks like that too, which is who I really am, Since you pierced my heart with your meanness.

Yet you, the murderer, look as bright, as clear,
As yonder Venus in her glimmering sphere.

And all the while you, the true murderer, look as beautiful As the planet Venus there in the sky, glimmering.

HERMIA
What's this to my Lysander? where is he?
Ah, good Demetrius, wilt thou give him me?

Why should I care about this as much as I care about Lysander? Where is he? Good Demetrius, please, will you give him to me?

DEMETRIUS
I had rather give his carcass to my hounds.

I'd rather give his dead body to my dogs.

HERMIA
Out, dog! out, cur! thou drivest me past the bounds
Of maiden's patience. Hast thou slain him, then?
Henceforth be never number'd among men!
O, once tell true, tell true, even for my sake!
Durst thou have look'd upon him being awake,
And hast thou kill'd him sleeping? O brave touch!
Could not a worm, an adder, do so much?
An adder did it; for with doubler tongue
Than thine, thou serpent, never adder stung.

*Get away from me you dog! You push me past the limits
Of any woman's patience. Have you killed him? From now on I will never consider you a man! For once, tell me the truth, for my sake! Would you dare to even look at him while he was awake, And then you killed him when he fell asleep? O, you are so brave! Even a worm or a snake could do that. And actually a snake did do it: for you have a more forked tongue Than any snake, and are more a snake than an actual snake.*

DEMETRIUS
You spend your passion on a misprised mood:
I am not guilty of Lysander's blood;
Nor is he dead, for aught that I can tell.

You are getting too passionate on something you have misunderstood: I am not guilty of killing Lysander – In fact, for all I know he isn't even dead.

HERMIA
I pray thee, tell me then that he is well.

Please then, tell me he is alright.

DEMETRIUS
An if I could, what should I get therefore?

And if I could, what would that get me?

HERMIA
A privilege never to see me more.
And from thy hated presence part I so:
See me no more, whether he be dead or no.

The privilege of never seeing me again. I am leaving your presence which I hate so much: Do not see me again, whether he is dead or not.

Exit

DEMETRIUS
There is no following her in this fierce vein:
Here therefore for a while I will remain.
So sorrow's heaviness doth heavier grow
For debt that bankrupt sleep doth sorrow owe:

I should not follow her while she is this angry, So I will stay here for a little. The weight of sorrow grows even heavier When one is behind on sleep.

Which now in some slight measure it will pay,
If for his tender here I make some stay.

*Now I'll get a little bit of that sleep back,
And sleep here to stave off the heaviness of
sorrow.*

Lies down and sleeps

OBERON
What hast thou done? thou hast mistaken quite
And laid the love-juice on some true-love's
sight:
Of thy misprision must perforce ensue
Some true love turn'd and not a false turn'd true.

*What have you done, Puck? You have
mistakenly Put the love potion on someone who
has true love.
Of your mistakes now what has happened
Is the changing of some true love, and not a
false love made true.*

PUCK
Then fate o'er-rules, that, one man holding troth,
A million fail, confounding oath on oath.

*Then it must be fate that made it so one man
who is truly in love fails his oaths like the
millions of others who naturally break these
oaths.*

OBERON
About the wood go swifter than the wind,
And Helena of Athens look thou find:
All fancy-sick she is and pale of cheer,
With sighs of love, that costs the fresh blood
dear:
By some illusion see thou bring her here:
I'll charm his eyes against she do appear.

*Go faster than the wind through the forest
And find Helena of Athens.
She will look sick from unrequited love, pale,
and joyless, Sighing from her pain, which makes
her pale.
Trick her into coming here
And I will enchant him with the potion for when
she gets here.*

PUCK
I go, I go; look how I go,
Swifter than arrow from the Tartar's bow.

*I go, I go, look how quickly I go,
Faster than an arrow shot by a Tartar.*

Exit

OBERON
Flower of this purple dye,
Hit with Cupid's archery,
Sink in apple of his eye.
When his love he doth espy,
Let her shine as gloriously
As the Venus of the sky.
When thou wakest, if she be by,
Beg of her for remedy.

*Purple flower,
Hit by an arrow of Cupid,
Sink into his eyes.
When he sees his love,
Let her be as beautiful
As the planet Venus up in the sky.
When you wake, if she is nearby,
Beg her to love you and cure the coming
lovesickness.*

Re-enter PUCK

PUCK
Captain of our fairy band,
Helena is here at hand;

*Captain of the fairies,
Helena is right here*

And the youth, mistook by me,
Pleading for a lover's fee.
Shall we their fond pageant see?
Lord, what fools these mortals be!

OBERON
Stand aside: the noise they make
Will cause Demetrius to awake.

PUCK
Then will two at once woo one;
That must needs be sport alone;
And those things do best please me
That befal preposterously.

LYSANDER
Why should you think that I should woo in scorn?
Scorn and derision never come in tears:
Look, when I vow, I weep; and vows so born,
In their nativity all truth appears.
How can these things in me seem scorn to you,
Bearing the badge of faith, to prove them true?

HELENA
You do advance your cunning more and more.
When truth kills truth, O devilish-holy fray!
These vows are Hermia's: will you give her o'er?
Weigh oath with oath, and you will nothing weigh:
Your vows to her and me, put in two scales,
Will even weigh, and both as light as tales.

LYSANDER
I had no judgment when to her I swore.

HELENA
Nor none, in my mind, now you give her o'er.

LYSANDER
Demetrius loves her, and he loves not you.

DEMETRIUS
[Awaking] O Helena, goddess, nymph, perfect, divine!

And the boy I mistook is here as well
Pleading for her love.
Shall we watch what they do?
Oh these humans are so foolish!

Stand here, the noise they make
Will wake up Demetrius.

Then two of them at once will be after one:
That is sport enough to watch.
These mishaps please me
From how preposterous they are.

Enter LYSANDER and HELENA

Why do you think I am mocking you when I woo you?
I wouldn't cry if I were making fun of you:
Look how I cry as I pledge my love – pledges like this Are born from honesty, and are thus true. How can you think that I am mocking you When these things wear the badge of faith, my tears, to prove that they are real?

You are becoming more and more cunning. What a horrible thing it is when true vows run against opposite true vows! Your promises to Hermia – will you break them? Two oaths on opposing scales will balance out and lead you to neither decision: Your promises to her, and now to me, Weigh evenly – and I think they are as empty as myths.

I was judging poorly when I swore my love to her.

And you have no judgment now, as you try to give her up.

Demetrius loves Hermia, anyway, he does not love you.

Oh Helena, goddess, fairy, perfect, divine!

To what, my love, shall I compare thine eyne?
Crystal is muddy. O, how ripe in show
Thy lips, those kissing cherries, tempting grow!
That pure congealed white, high Taurus snow,
Fann'd with the eastern wind, turns to a crow
When thou hold'st up thy hand: O, let me kiss
This princess of pure white, this seal of bliss!

HELENA
O spite! O hell! I see you all are bent
To set against me for your merriment:
If you were civil and knew courtesy,
You would not do me thus much injury.
Can you not hate me, as I know you do,
But you must join in souls to mock me too?
If you were men, as men you are in show,
You would not use a gentle lady so;
To vow, and swear, and superpraise my parts,
When I am sure you hate me with your hearts.
You both are rivals, and love Hermia;
And now both rivals, to mock Helena:
A trim exploit, a manly enterprise,
To conjure tears up in a poor maid's eyes
With your derision! none of noble sort
Would so offend a virgin, and extort
A poor soul's patience, all to make you sport.

LYSANDER
You are unkind, Demetrius; be not so;
For you love Hermia; this you know I know:
And here, with all good will, with all my heart,
In Hermia's love I yield you up my part;
And yours of Helena to me bequeath,
Whom I do love and will do till my death.

HELENA
Never did mockers waste more idle breath.

DEMETRIUS
Lysander, keep thy Hermia; I will none:
If e'er I loved her, all that love is gone.
My heart to her but as guest-wise sojourn'd,
And now to Helen is it home return'd,
There to remain.

LYSANDER

*What can I compare your beauty to?
Crystal is muddy. Oh your lips
so ripe, like two cherries touching each other,
are so tempting! The pure whiteness of a
mountaintop's snow Blown by the eastern wind
turns as black as a crow When compared with
your hand. Let me kiss You, a princess of pure
white, and seal my happiness!*

*Oh curses on both of you! You are both together
Joined in mocking me for your own enjoyment.
If you were kind, and new common courtesy,
You wouldn't hurt me this much.
Can you just hate me, as I know you do,
Without joining together to make fun of me as
well? If you were true men, as noble as you
pretend to be You would not treat a gentle lady
like this: To promise and swear your love, to
overemphasize my beauty, When I know that
really you hate me in your hearts. You are rivals
in loving Hermia, And now you are rivals in
mocking me: A neat and manly goal,
To create tears to fall from a poor girl's eyes
From your evilness! No truly noble man
Would cause such hurt in a young, chaste girl,
none would test A poor soul's patience for his
own fun.*

*You are mean, Demetrius, now stop.
You love Hermia and you know that I know it,
And right here, with the best of my intentions,
I give up my pursuit of Hermia.
Now you give up your vows to Helena
Whom I love and will do so until I die.*

*Jokers never wasted so much breath in speaking
nonsense.*

*Lysander, keep your Hermia because I will not.
If I ever truly lover her, that love is now gone.
My heart journeyed to her, but did not stay,
And now it has come back to its home, Helena,
Where it will remain.*

Helen, it is not so.

DEMETRIUS
Disparage not the faith thou dost not know,
Lest, to thy peril, thou aby it dear.
Look, where thy love comes; yonder is thy dear.

HERMIA
Dark night, that from the eye his function takes,
The ear more quick of apprehension makes;
Wherein it doth impair the seeing sense,
It pays the hearing double recompense.
Thou art not by mine eye, Lysander, found;
Mine ear, I thank it, brought me to thy sound
But why unkindly didst thou leave me so?

LYSANDER
Why should he stay, whom love doth press to
go?

HERMIA
What love could press Lysander from my side?

LYSANDER
Lysander's love, that would not let him bide,
Fair Helena, who more engilds the night
Than all you fiery oes and eyes of light.
Why seek'st thou me? could not this make thee
know,
The hate I bear thee made me leave thee so?

HERMIA
You speak not as you think: it cannot be.

HELENA
Lo, she is one of this confederacy!
Now I perceive they have conjoin'd all three
To fashion this false sport, in spite of me.
Injurious Hermia! most ungrateful maid!
Have you conspired, have you with these
contrived
To bait me with this foul derision?
Is all the counsel that we two have shared,
The sisters' vows, the hours that we have spent,

Helena, he is lying.

*Don't insult the love you do not know
Or else, to your harm, you will have to pay for
your words. Look, your love is coming from over
there; there is your beloved.*

Re-enter HERMIA

*The night is so dark that it ruins the eye's ability
to see, But it makes the ear's hearing stronger.
Though it hurts one's sense of sight,
It accounts for such harm by giving hearing
twice as much perception. I could not find you,
Lysander, by my sight, But I thank my ears that
brought me to your voice – Why did you so
abruptly leave my side?*

*Why should I have stayed, when love pressed me
to go?*

*What love could possibly press you to go and
outweigh your love for me?*

*My unabiding love for
Beautiful Helena, who makes the night look
more golden Than do the stars above.
Why did you look for me? Didn't my leaving
make it obvious
That I hate you, and that this hate made me
leave?*

You cannot be speaking what you really think.

*Hermia is part of this plan to mock me!
Now I see that all three have joined together
To play this mean joke at my expense.
Hurtful Hermia! You awful lady!
Have you planned with these men
To trick me with this mean ploy?
Remember all that we shared, the conversations
And the promises, the hours spent together,
We were even angry that we didn't have more*

When we have chid the hasty-footed time
For parting us,--O, is it all forgot?
All school-days' friendship, childhood
innocence?
We, Hermia, like two artificial gods,
Have with our needles created both one flower,
Both on one sampler, sitting on one cushion,
Both warbling of one song, both in one key,
As if our hands, our sides, voices and minds,
Had been incorporate. So we grow together,
Like to a double cherry, seeming parted,
But yet an union in partition;
Two lovely berries moulded on one stem;
So, with two seeming bodies, but one heart;
Two of the first, like coats in heraldry,
Due but to one and crowned with one crest.
And will you rent our ancient love asunder,
To join with men in scorning your poor friend?
It is not friendly, 'tis not maidenly:
Our sex, as well as I, may chide you for it,
Though I alone do feel the injury.

HERMIA
I am amazed at your passionate words.
I scorn you not: it seems that you scorn me.

HELENA
Have you not set Lysander, as in scorn,
To follow me and praise my eyes and face?
And made your other love, Demetrius,
Who even but now did spurn me with his foot,
To call me goddess, nymph, divine and rare,
Precious, celestial? Wherefore speaks he this
To her he hates? and wherefore doth Lysander
Deny your love, so rich within his soul,
And tender me, forsooth, affection,
But by your setting on, by your consent?
What thought I be not so in grace as you,
So hung upon with love, so fortunate,
But miserable most, to love unloved?
This you should pity rather than despise.

HERNIA
I understand not what you mean by this.

Time together – and now is it all lost?
Our friendship at school and our young
innocent friendship, lost?
Hermia, we used to be like fake gods of our
world,
Sitting together and sewing the same flower
On the same sampler, sitting on the same
cushion and singing together in the same key,
As if our hands and bodies, our voices and our
minds Were fused together. We grew together
Like two cherries – seemingly apart,
But united at the base,
Two lovely cherries joined at the stem.
Seemingly we had two different bodies, but
always one heart, Like two coats of arms on a
shield That pledge their allegiance to the same
king, crowned with a single crest. And now will
you break the bonds of all of this By joining with
these men in mocking me? It is neither friendly
nor ladylike: All women would do well to
criticize you for it, Though I am the only woman
hurt by it.

What you are saying stuns me.
I do not hold you in contempt, but it seems you
think of me that way.

Didn't you make Lysander, from your contempt
for me, Follow me and compliment my looks?
And then didn't you make the other man who
loves you, Demetrius, Who at all times before
now turned me away, even with his foot, Call me
a goddess, a fairy, divine and rare, Precious
and heavenly? Why else would he say this To
the one he hates? And why does Lysander Deny
his love for you, which before was all he could
talk about, And now give me, really, signs of
affection – Why else but from you consenting to
it and asking him to do it? What did you think,
seeing me in such an unhappy position, So
obsessed with love, so happy to be in love But
all the more miserable to be in love without
being loved in return? You should pity me
instead of mock me.

I don't know what you mean by what you are

52

HELENA
Ay, do, persever, counterfeit sad looks,
Make mouths upon me when I turn my back;
Wink each at other; hold the sweet jest up:
This sport, well carried, shall be chronicled.
If you have any pity, grace, or manners,
You would not make me such an argument.
But fare ye well: 'tis partly my own fault;
Which death or absence soon shall remedy.

*Fine, continue your fake sadness,
And laugh silently at me when I turn around,
Wink at each other, keep up your joke.
This game, carried out long enough, will be
remembered. If you have any pity, grace, or
manners, You would not make me even have to
appeal like this. But have fun – it's all partly my
own fault I guess, And death or running away
will fix it soon enough.*

LYSANDER
Stay, gentle Helena; hear my excuse:
My love, my life my soul, fair Helena!

*Wait, Helena, hear what I have to say,
Dear love, the life of my soul, beautiful Helena!*

HELENA
O excellent!

Great, more joking.

HERMIA
Sweet, do not scorn her so.

Darling, do not mock her like that.

DEMETRIUS
If she cannot entreat, I can compel.

*If Hermia can't get you to stop, I can force you
to.*

LYSANDER
Thou canst compel no more than she entreat:
Thy threats have no more strength than her weak
prayers.
Helen, I love thee; by my life, I do:
I swear by that which I will lose for thee,
To prove him false that says I love thee not.

*Your forcing will have no more strength than
Hermia's pleas. Your threats are not stronger
than her prayers.
Helena, I swear by my life that I love you,
And will lose that life for you,
Just to prove Demetrius wrong who says I do
not love you.*

DEMETRIUS
I say I love thee more than he can do.

I say I love you more than Lysander does.

LYSANDER
If thou say so, withdraw, and prove it too.

*If you think so, then draw your sword and prove
it.*

DEMETRIUS
Quick, come!

Alright, come!

HERMIA
Lysander, whereto tends all this?

Lysander, why are you doing all of this?

LYSANDER
Away, you Ethiope!

Get away from me, African woman!

DEMETRIUS
No, no; he'll
Seem to break loose; take on as you would follow,
But yet come not: you are a tame man, go!

*No, he'll
Pretend to leave you, Hermia. And you
Lysander will pretend to fight
But will not advance toward me. You are a
cowardly man, go away!*

LYSANDER
Hang off, thou cat, thou burr! vile thing, let loose,
Or I will shake thee from me like a serpent!

*Get off of me, you cat, you thorn! Awful thing,
let go of me,
Hermia, or I will shake you off as if you are a
serpent!*

HERMIA
Why are you grown so rude? what change is this?
Sweet love,--

*Why have you become so mean? What changed?
My love--*

LYSANDER
Thy love! out, tawny Tartar, out!
Out, loathed medicine! hated potion, hence!

*Your love! No, get away, you black skinned
Tartar! Out, evil medicine, hated potion!*

HERMIA
Do you not jest?

Are you not joking?

HELENA
Yes, sooth; and so do you.

Yes, of course he is, and you are as well.

LYSANDER
Demetrius, I will keep my word with thee.

Demetrius, I will duel you now.

DEMETRIUS
I would I had your bond, for I perceive
A weak bond holds you: I'll not trust your word.

*I wish I believed your bond, for I see
That you seem to make promises you break
easily, so I won't trust your word.*

LYSANDER
What, should I hurt her, strike her, kill her dead?
Although I hate her, I'll not harm her so.

*What must I do, hurt Hermia? Hit her? Kill her?
Though I hate her, I will not do that.*

HERMIA
What, can you do me greater harm than hate?
Hate me! wherefore? O me! what news, my love!
Am not I Hermia? are not you Lysander?
I am as fair now as I was erewhile.
Since night you loved me; yet since night you left me:
Why, then you left me--O, the gods forbid!--

*What harm can you do to me that is greater than
hate? Hate me! Why? Oh my! What has
happened, my love?
Aren't I Hermia? Aren't you Lysander?
I am just as beautiful as I was before.
Since the night started you still loved me, but
then you left me:
Then you left me-- Oh God forbid!--*

In earnest, shall I say?

Did you really? Must I admit that?

LYSANDER
Ay, by my life;
And never did desire to see thee more.
Therefore be out of hope, of question, of doubt;
Be certain, nothing truer; 'tis no jest
That I do hate thee and love Helena.

Yes, I did,
And I do not wish to see you again.
Stop questioning and stop wondering, stop
hoping: Be certain, because nothing is more
true than this: I am not joking That I hate you
and love Helena.

HERMIA
O me! you juggler! you canker-blossom!
You thief of love! what, have you come by night
And stolen my love's heart from him?

Oh my! Helena, you awful thorn!
You thief! Did you come in the night
And steal Lysander's heart from me?

HELENA
Fine, i'faith!
Have you no modesty, no maiden shame,
No touch of bashfulness? What, will you tear
Impatient answers from my gentle tongue?
Fie, fie! you counterfeit, you puppet, you!

That's a nice touch.
Have you no shame at all,
No slight remorse? Are you trying to make me
angry In order to get me to say impatient and
evil things? Damn you! You fake, you puppet!

HERMIA
Puppet? why so? ay, that way goes the game.
Now I perceive that she hath made compare
Between our statures; she hath urged her height;
And with her personage, her tall personage,
Her height, forsooth, she hath prevail'd with
him.
And are you grown so high in his esteem;
Because I am so dwarfish and so low?
How low am I, thou painted maypole? speak;
How low am I? I am not yet so low
But that my nails can reach unto thine eyes.

Puppet? Why that? Oh now I see.
Helena has compared
Our heights, and, taller, has praised her own
height: Because she is tall, taller than me,
She has convinced Lysander to love her instead.
Did you grow in his eyes because of this?
Because I am so short, like a dwarf, and thus a
person of lower quality? Well how low of a
person am I, you who is as tall as a maypole?
I know this much: I am not so short
That I cannot scratch your eyes out with my
nails.

HELENA
I pray you, though you mock me, gentlemen,
Let her not hurt me: I was never curst;
I have no gift at all in shrewishness;
I am a right maid for my cowardice:
Let her not strike me. You perhaps may think,
Because she is something lower than myself,
That I can match her.

Please, men, though you are making fun of me,
Don't let her hurt me. I was never cursed at
And am not good at being an evil woman.
It is better that I am a coward,
But let her not hit me. You may think that
Because she is shorter
I can fight her off.

HERMIA
Lower! hark, again.

See! She says "shorter" again.

HELENA
Good Hermia, do not be so bitter with me.
I evermore did love you, Hermia,
Did ever keep your counsels, never wrong'd
you;
Save that, in love unto Demetrius,
I told him of your stealth unto this wood.
He follow'd you; for love I follow'd him;
But he hath chid me hence and threaten'd me
To strike me, spurn me, nay, to kill me too:
And now, so you will let me quiet go,
To Athens will I bear my folly back
And follow you no further: let me go:
You see how simple and how fond I am.

Hermia, do not be bitter with me.
I have always loved you, Hermia,
Always kept your secrets, never wronged you,
Until this: because of my love for Demetrius
I told him of your plans to run away into the
forest.
He followed you and for love I followed him,
But then he turned me away and threatened
To hit me, no, even to kill me.
Now, let me quietly go away,
Back to Athens where I will bring my mistakes
with me And will not follow you anymore. Let
me go, You see see how simple and foolishly in
love I am.

HERMIA
Why, get you gone: who is't that hinders you?

Then go: what keeps you here?

HELENA
A foolish heart, that I leave here behind.

A foolish heart that I must force myself to give
up.

HERMIA
What, with Lysander?

Your love for Lysander?

HELENA
With Demetrius.

For Demetrius.

LYSANDER
Be not afraid; she shall not harm thee, Helena.

Do not fear, Helena, Hermia will not hurt you.

DEMETRIUS
No, sir, she shall not, though you take her part.

No, she won't, even if you, Lysander, try to help
her.

HELENA
O, when she's angry, she is keen and shrewd!
She was a vixen when she went to school;
And though she be but little, she is fierce.

Oh, she is so smart and vicious when she is
angry! She was a vixen at school,
And though she is little, she can be fierce.

HERMIA
'Little' again! nothing but 'low' and 'little'!
Why will you suffer her to flout me thus?
Let me come to her.

"Little" again! You keep saying "low" and
"little"! Why do you both allow her to mock me
like this? Let me get to her.

LYSANDER
Get you gone, you dwarf;
You minimus, of hindering knot-grass made;

Go away, you dwarf,
You miniature thing made of grass,

You bead, you acorn.

You bead, you acorn.

DEMETRIUS
You are too officious
In her behalf that scorns your services.
Let her alone: speak not of Helena;
Take not her part; for, if thou dost intend
Never so little show of love to her,
Thou shalt aby it.

That is going to far,
Especially for one who does not want your love
or aid. Let Helena alone, do not speak for her
And stop taking Helena's side. If you continue
To treat Hermia so poorly,
You'll pay for it.

LYSANDER
Now she holds me not;
Now follow, if thou darest, to try whose right,
Of thine or mine, is most in Helena.

Hermia is nothing to me now.
Now, if you dare, follow me and let us see whose
right, Yours or mine, is Helena's love.

DEMETRIUS
Follow! nay, I'll go with thee, cheek by jole.

I will not follow – I will walk side by side with
you.

Exeunt LYSANDER and DEMETRIUS

HERMIA
You, mistress, all this coil is 'long of you:
Nay, go not back.

All of this fighting is because of you, Helena,
Do not go back to Athens.

HELENA
I will not trust you, I,
Nor longer stay in your curst company.
Your hands than mine are quicker for a fray,
My legs are longer though, to run away.

I don't trust you, and I
Will no longer stay here in your awful company.
You are more desirous of a fight,
But my long legs are better for running away.

Exit

HERMIA
I am amazed, and know not what to say.

I am amazed, and don't know what to say.

Exit

OBERON
This is thy negligence: still thou mistakest,
Or else committ'st thy knaveries wilfully.

This is your fault: either you made a mistake
Or you are playing a prank on purpose.

PUCK
Believe me, king of shadows, I mistook.
Did not you tell me I should know the man
By the Athenian garment be had on?
And so far blameless proves my enterprise,
That I have 'nointed an Athenian's eyes;
And so far am I glad it so did sort

Believe me, my king, I made a mistake.
Remember that you told me I would recognize
the man By his Athenian clothing?
So far, I have done nothing wrong,
Since I put the potion on an Athenian man's
eyes. Though I am glad it all turned out like this,

As this their jangling I esteem a sport.

Since I find their fighting a fun game to watch.

OBERON
Thou see'st these lovers seek a place to fight:
Hie therefore, Robin, overcast the night;
The starry welkin cover thou anon
With drooping fog as black as Acheron,
And lead these testy rivals so astray
As one come not within another's way.
Like to Lysander sometime frame thy tongue,
Then stir Demetrius up with bitter wrong;
And sometime rail thou like Demetrius;
And from each other look thou lead them thus,
Till o'er their brows death-counterfeiting sleep
With leaden legs and batty wings doth creep:
Then crush this herb into Lysander's eye;
Whose liquor hath this virtuous property,
To take from thence all error with his might,
And make his eyeballs roll with wonted sight.
When they next wake, all this derision
Shall seem a dream and fruitless vision,
And back to Athens shall the lovers wend,
With league whose date till death shall never
end.
Whiles I in this affair do thee employ,
I'll to my queen and beg her Indian boy;
And then I will her charmed eye release
From monster's view, and all things shall be
peace.

You saw as well as I did that the men are
looking for a place to fight, So go, Puck, and
make the night cloudy. Cover the starry sky
With a low fog as dark as the Acheron River,
And make these fighting men lose each other
So they do not end up dueling.
Sometimes speak like Lysander
And get Demetrius angry at being wronged,
And sometimes speak like Demetrius.
Like this keep them away from each other
Until they fall asleep, appearing almost like they
are dead. Then, creep quietly up to them with
bat's wings And put this antidote into
Lysander's eye Which will, by it's good
qualities, Remove the former potion
And make his eyes return to their natural sight.
When they wake back up, all of this fighting
Shall seem like a dream with no aftereffects,
And the lovers shall go back to Athens
With their beloveds in order to marry them.
While you do this job,
I will go to Queen Titania and ask for her Indian
boy
And then will give her eye the antidote so that
she stops Loving the monster, and finally all
things will be peaceful.

PUCK
My fairy lord, this must be done with haste,
For night's swift dragons cut the clouds full fast,
And yonder shines Aurora's harbinger;
At whose approach, ghosts, wandering here and
there,
Troop home to churchyards: damned spirits all,
That in crossways and floods have burial,
Already to their wormy beds are gone;
For fear lest day should look their shames upon,
They willfully themselves exile from light
And must for aye consort with black-brow'd
night.

My king, this should be done quickly
Since night is already fading quickly
And far in the east the morning appears to be
breaking. When that happens, the ghosts that
wander about Return to their homes in the
graveyards, these damned spirits
Who were not buried in holy grounds
Have already returned to their wormy graves.
They are afraid that day will look at their shame
So they choose to stay away from the light
And instead only come out at night.

OBERON
But we are spirits of another sort:

We are different spirits than them.

I with the morning's love have oft made sport,
And, like a forester, the groves may tread,
Even till the eastern gate, all fiery-red,
Opening on Neptune with fair blessed beams,
Turns into yellow gold his salt green streams.
But, notwithstanding, haste; make no delay:
We may effect this business yet ere day.

I have often played in the morning with the morning's blessing And am allowed, like a hunter, to walk through the forests Even until the east is as red as fire And the sun rises over the oceans, its blessed beams Turning the salty green seawater golden yellow. In any case, hurry along So that we can finish this work before day starts.

Exit

PUCK
Up and down, up and down,
I will lead them up and down:
I am fear'd in field and town:
Goblin, lead them up and down.
Here comes one.

Up and down, and back and forth, I will lead them all over. Those who live in the town and the fields are afraid of me. I am Goblin who will lead them all over. Here is one now.

Re-enter LYSANDER

LYSANDER
Where art thou, proud Demetrius? speak thou now.

Where are you, Demetrius? Tell me.

PUCK
Here, villain; drawn and ready. Where art thou?

Here, you villain, with my sword ready. Where are you?

LYSANDER
I will be with thee straight.

I will be near you soon enough.

PUCK
Follow me, then,
To plainer ground.

Follow me, then, To a good ground for battle.

Exit LYSANDER, as following the voice

Re-enter DEMETRIUS

DEMETRIUS
Lysander! speak again:
Thou runaway, thou coward, art thou fled?
Speak! In some bush? Where dost thou hide thy head?

Lysander, speak! You coward, have you run away? Speak! Are you hiding in a bush? Where?

PUCK
Thou coward, art thou bragging to the stars,
Telling the bushes that thou look'st for wars,
And wilt not come? Come, recreant; come, thou child;

You coward, are you bragging to the heavens And telling all of the bushes that you are ready to fight, But will not come at me? Come, miscreant, come you child.

I'll whip thee with a rod: he is defiled
That draws a sword on thee.

DEMETRIUS
Yea, art thou there?

PUCK
Follow my voice: we'll try no manhood here.

*I will beat you with a stick. Whoever
Pulls a sword on me will become insulted.*

Hey, where are you?

Follow my voice, we will not fight here.

Exeunt

Re-enter LYSANDER

LYSANDER
He goes before me and still dares me on:
When I come where he calls, then he is gone.
The villain is much lighter-heel'd than I:
I follow'd fast, but faster he did fly;
That fallen am I in dark uneven way,
And here will rest me.

Come, thou gentle day!
For if but once thou show me thy grey light,
I'll find Demetrius and revenge this spite.

Lies down

Sleeps

Re-enter PUCK and DEMETRIUS

PUCK
Ho, ho, ho! Coward, why comest thou not?

Ha ha! Coward, why haven't you come yet?

DEMETRIUS
Abide me, if thou darest; for well I wot
Thou runn'st before me, shifting every place,
And darest not stand, nor look me in the face.
Where art thou now?

*Stay where you are, if you dare. I see
You running ahead of me, changing your place,
Because you do not dare stop and stand up to
me. Now where are you?*

PUCK
Come hither: I am here.

Come over here, I am here.

DEMETRIUS
Nay, then, thou mock'st me. Thou shalt buy this dear,
If ever I thy face by daylight see:
Now, go thy way. Faintness constraineth me
To measure out my length on this cold bed.
By day's approach look to be visited.

*No, you are mocking me. You will pay for this
If I ever see you in the daylight.
Go along, I am too tired and must
Stretch out on the ground to sleep.
Prepare yourself to fight in the morning.*

Lies down and sleeps

HELENA

O weary night, O long and tedious night,
Abate thy hour! Shine comforts from the east,
That I may back to Athens by daylight,
From these that my poor company detest:
And sleep, that sometimes shuts up sorrow's eye,
Steal me awhile from mine own company.

PUCK

Yet but three? Come one more;
Two of both kinds make up four.
Here she comes, curst and sad:
Cupid is a knavish lad,
Thus to make poor females mad.

HERMIA

Never so weary, never so in woe,
Bedabbled with the dew and torn with briers,
I can no further crawl, no further go;
My legs can keep no pace with my desires.
Here will I rest me till the break of day.
Heavens shield Lysander, if they mean a fray!

PUCK

On the ground
Sleep sound:
I'll apply
To your eye,
Gentle lover, remedy.

When thou wakest,
Thou takest
True delight
In the sight
Of thy former lady's eye:
And the country proverb known,
That every man should take his own,
In your waking shall be shown:

Re-enter HELENA

*Oh night that has been so long and tedious,
Please end! Let the daylight break from the east
So that I can get back to Athens easily
And leave these supposed friends who really
hate me. Now I will sleep, and hope that sleep
can quell my sorrow
By removing me from myself for a little.*

Lies down and sleeps

*I've seen only three so far, where is the other?
Two men and two women make four for the
company. Here comes Hermia, cursed and sad:
Cupid is a mean prankster
To women feel this poorly.*

Re-enter HERMIA

*I have never been this exhausted or this sad,
And I am wet with dew, and scratched by the
thorns. I cannot crawl any farther, much less
walk. My legs are not as strong as my desire to
get back to Athens, So I will rest here for the
rest of the night, until morning. God protect
Lysander if there is a duel!*

Lies down and sleeps

*Sleep here
On the ground
While I put this potion
In your eye,
Gentle lover, and it will fix you.*

Squeezing the juice on LYSANDER's eyes

*When you wake,
You will feel
Your true love again
After you see
Hermia, whom you formerly loved.
The saying in the country
That "Every man should take his own,"
And you will prove this when you wake:*

Jack shall have Jill;
Nought shall go ill;
The man shall have his mare again, and all shall
be well.

Jack will love Jill
And neither shall be upset,
The man will have his lady again, and
everything will be good.

Exit

Act IV

Scene I

The same. LYSANDER, DEMETRIUS, HELENA, and HERMIA lying asleep.

Enter TITANIA and BOTTOM; PEASEBLOSSOM, COBWEB, MOTH, MUSTARDSEED, and other Fairies attending; OBERON behind unseen

TITANIA
Come, sit thee down upon this flowery bed,
While I thy amiable cheeks do coy,
And stick musk-roses in thy sleek smooth head,
And kiss thy fair large ears, my gentle joy.

Come over here and sit on this bed of flowers
While I brush your smooth cheeks
And places flowers in your hair
And kiss your beautiful, large ears, my joy.

BOTTOM
Where's Peaseblossom?

Where's Peaseblossom?

PEASEBLOSSOM
Ready.

Here.

BOTTOM
Scratch my head Peaseblossom. Where's
Mounsieur Cobweb?

Please scratch my head, Peaseblossom. And
where is Monsieur Cobweb?

COBWEB
Ready.

Here.

BOTTOM
Mounsieur Cobweb, good mounsieur, get you your
weapons in your hand, and kill me a red-hipped
humble-bee on the top of a thistle; and, good
mounsieur, bring me the honey-bag. Do not fret
yourself too much in the action, mounsieur; and,
good mounsieur, have a care the honey-bag
break not;
I would be loath to have you overflown with a
honey-bag, signior. Where's Mounsieur
Mustardseed?

Monsieur Cobweb, good monsieur, fetch
your weapons and kill a red-striped
bumblebee sitting on the top of a thistle for me,
and then,
monsieur, bring me honey from it. Do not worry
too much while you are doing this, monsieur,
and, good monsieur, try not to break the honey
bag:
I would hate to see you covered with
honey, signior. Where's Monsieur Mustardseed?

MUSTARDSEED
Ready.

Here.

BOTTOM

Give me your neaf, Mounsieur Mustardseed.
Pray you,
leave your courtesy, good mounsieur.

Give me your hand, Monsieur Mustardseed.
Please,
do what I ask, good monsieur.

MUSTARDSEED

What's your Will?

What would you like me to do?

BOTTOM

Nothing, good mounsieur, but to help Cavalery
Cobweb
to scratch. I must to the barber's, monsieur; for
methinks I am marvellous hairy about the face;
and I
am such a tender ass, if my hair do but tickle
me,
I must scratch.

Nothing, good monsieur, except to help Calvary
Cobweb
scratch my head. I must go to a barber,
monsieur, because I think my beard has grown
out all around my face,
and my face is so tender that if hair only tickles
it slightly,
I must scratch it.

TITANIA

What, wilt thou hear some music,
my sweet love?

Would you like to hear some music,
my love?

BOTTOM

I have a reasonable good ear in music. Let's
have
the tongs and the bones.

I have a good ear for music. Someone play
The triangle and the keys.

TITANIA

Or say, sweet love, what thou desirest to eat.

Or maybe, my love, you can say what you would
like to eat.

BOTTOM

Truly, a peck of provender: I could munch your
good
dry oats. Methinks I have a great desire to a
bottle
of hay: good hay, sweet hay, hath no fellow.

Really, a good bit of grass: I could munch on
some
dry oats. I think I really want a portion
of hay. There is nothing like good, sweet hay.

TITANIA

I have a venturous fairy that shall seek
The squirrel's hoard, and fetch thee new nuts.

I have a fairy that will find
The nuts a squirrel has hidden for winter, and
will fetch you some of them.

BOTTOM

I had rather have a handful or two of dried peas.
But, I pray you, let none of your people stir me:
I
have an exposition of sleep come upon me.

I'd rather eat a handful or two of dried peas.
But, please, don't let your fairies wait on me
now: I
am feeling incredibly tired all of a sudden.

TITANIA
Sleep thou, and I will wind thee in my arms.
Fairies, begone, and be all ways away.

So doth the woodbine the sweet honeysuckle
Gently entwist; the female ivy so
Enrings the barky fingers of the elm.
O, how I love thee! how I dote on thee!

OBERON
[Advancing] Welcome, good Robin.
See'st thou this sweet sight?
Her dotage now I do begin to pity:
For, meeting her of late behind the wood,
Seeking sweet favours from this hateful fool,
I did upbraid her and fall out with her;
For she his hairy temples then had rounded
With a coronet of fresh and fragrant flowers;
And that same dew, which sometime on the buds
Was wont to swell like round and orient pearls,
Stood now within the pretty flowerets' eyes
Like tears that did their own disgrace bewail.
When I had at my pleasure taunted her
And she in mild terms begg'd my patience,
I then did ask of her her changeling child;
Which straight she gave me, and her fairy sent
To bear him to my bower in fairy land.
And now I have the boy, I will undo
This hateful imperfection of her eyes:
And, gentle Puck, take this transformed scalp
From off the head of this Athenian swain;
That, he awaking when the other do,
May all to Athens back again repair
And think no more of this night's accidents
But as the fierce vexation of a dream.
But first I will release the fairy queen.
Be as thou wast wont to be;
See as thou wast wont to see:
Dian's bud o'er Cupid's flower

Then sleep, and I will put my arms around you.
Fairies, go away in all directions.

Exeunt fairies

The woodbine plant and the honeysuckle
Wrap around each other just as I am doing to
you. So does the female ivy Wrapping around
the bark trunk of the elm. I love you so much
and want to give you so much!

They sleep

Enter PUCK

Hello, good Robin.
Do you see this sweet picture?
I'm starting to pity her affection
Because, when I met her recently here in the
forest, She was looking for gifts for this fool,
And I argued and fought with her.
She has placed around his hairy head
A crown of fresh, good smelling flowers:
And the dew that rests on the flower buds,
Which sometimes looks like perfectly round
pearls from the Far East,
Stood in the flowers
Like tears, crying at the disgrace of being
around the fool's head. When I was done having
my fun in taunting her And she had begged me
to stop, I asked her of her orphan child
Whom she immediately gave to me, and sent her
fairy To take him to my room in fairy land.
Now that I have the boy I will give her the
antidote To remove this ugly infatuation.
Also, Puck, remove this donkey-head
From the head of the Athenian commoner
So that he, waking up when the others do,
Can return to Athens again
And think nothing of the night's adventures,
Regarding them only as a dream.
First, I will cure Queen Titania.
Be as you were
And see how you used to see:
This flower of Diana's, the goddess of Virginity,

Hath such force and blessed power.
Now, my Titania; wake you, my sweet queen.

TITANIA
My Oberon! what visions have I seen!
Methought I was enamour'd of an ass.

OBERON
There lies your love.

TITANIA
How came these things to pass?
O, how mine eyes do loathe his visage now!

OBERON
Silence awhile. Robin, take off this head.
Titania, music call; and strike more dead
Than common sleep of all these five the sense.

TITANIA
Music, ho! music, such as charmeth sleep!

PUCK
Now, when thou wakest, with thine
own fool's eyes peep.

OBERON
Sound, music! Come, my queen, take hands
with me,
And rock the ground whereon these sleepers be.
Now thou and I are new in amity,
And will to-morrow midnight solemnly
Dance in Duke Theseus' house triumphantly,
And bless it to all fair prosperity:
There shall the pairs of faithful lovers be
Wedded, with Theseus, all in jollity.

PUCK
Fairy king, attend, and mark:
I do hear the morning lark.

OBERON
Then, my queen, in silence sad,
Trip we after the night's shade:
We the globe can compass soon,

*against the flower struck by Cupid's arrow, Has
the blessed power to turn you to normal. Now,
Titania, wake up, my queen.*

*Oberon! What dreams I have had!
I thought I was in love with a donkey.*

Right there is who you loved.

*How did these things happen?
Oh, I can't stand the sight of him now.*

*Be quiet for a moment. Robin, remove the false
head. Titania, call for music, the kind that will
make these people Sleep more soundly than the
dead.*

Play music, fairies! The kind that creates sleep!

Music, still

*Now when you wake, you
will look out with your human, but still foolish,
eyes.*

*Play, music! Come with me, my queen, hold my
hand
And dance with me to keep the sleepers alseep.
We are friendly again
And tomorrow at midnight
We will dance in Duke Theseus' house in
celebration, Blessing it for success.
And there, these pairs of faithful lovers
Will be married as well, along with Theseus, in
happiness.*

*King Oberon, listen –
I do hear the morning bird.*

*In that case, my queen, let us silently
Leave to wherever it is still night.
We can go around the world*

Swifter than the wandering moon.

Quicker than the moon does.

TITANIA
Come, my lord, and in our flight
Tell me how it came this night
That I sleeping here was found
With these mortals on the ground.

Come, my king, and while we travel
Tell me what happened this night,
How I was sleeping here
With these humans on the ground next to me.

Exeunt
Horns winded within

Enter THESEUS, HIPPOLYTA, EGEUS, and train

THESEUS
Go, one of you, find out the forester;
For now our observation is perform'd;
And since we have the vaward of the day,
My love shall hear the music of my hounds.
Uncouple in the western valley; let them go:
Dispatch, I say, and find the forester.

One of you, go and find the forest manager.
Since we have finished our May Day rites
And now have the beginning of the day in front
of us, My love will hear the sound of hunting
horns for my dogs. Untie them in the valley and
let them go. I said leave and find the forest
manager.

Exit an Attendant

We will, fair queen, up to the mountain's top,
And mark the musical confusion
Of hounds and echo in conjunction.

We will go, beautiful queen, up to the mountain
peak And listen to the confusing sounds
Of dogs barking and their barks echoing back.

HIPPOLYTA
I was with Hercules and Cadmus once,
When in a wood of Crete they bay'd the bear
With hounds of Sparta: never did I hear
Such gallant chiding: for, besides the groves,
The skies, the fountains, every region near
Seem'd all one mutual cry: I never heard
So musical a discord, such sweet thunder.

I was with Hercules and Cadmus once
In a forest in Crete and their Spartan dogs
Surrounded a bear: I never heard
Such impressive barking. Besides the forest,
The skies and fountains, and everywhere around
us Seemed to echo the barking in unison. I never
heard Such beautiful noise, such sweet thunder.

THESEUS
My hounds are bred out of the Spartan kind,
So flew'd, so sanded, and their heads are hung
With ears that sweep away the morning dew;
Crook-knee'd, and dew-lapp'd like Thessalian
bulls;
Slow in pursuit, but match'd in mouth like bells,
Each under each. A cry more tuneable
Was never holla'd to, nor cheer'd with horn,

My hounds are bred from Spartan ones,
With the same hanging lips and sandy colored
coat, and their heads similarly hang With their
ears low along the morning dew. They similarly
have crooked knees, and neck folds like bulls
from Thessaly. They are slower in the chase, but
they have the same bark, like bells In their
mouths. There was never a better sounding cry

In Crete, in Sparta, nor in Thessaly:
Judge when you hear. But, soft! what nymphs
are these?

EGEUS
My lord, this is my daughter here asleep;
And this, Lysander; this Demetrius is;
This Helena, old Nedar's Helena:
I wonder of their being here together.

THESEUS
No doubt they rose up early to observe
The rite of May, and hearing our intent,
Came here in grace our solemnity.
But speak, Egeus; is not this the day
That Hermia should give answer of her choice?

EGEUS
It is, my lord.

THESEUS
Go, bid the huntsmen wake them with their
horns.

Good morrow, friends. Saint Valentine is past:
Begin these wood-birds but to couple now?

LYSANDER
Pardon, my lord.

THESEUS
I pray you all, stand up.
I know you two are rival enemies:
How comes this gentle concord in the world,
That hatred is so far from jealousy,
To sleep by hate, and fear no enmity?

LYSANDER
My lord, I shall reply amazedly,
Half sleep, half waking: but as yet, I swear,
I cannot truly say how I came here;
But, as I think,--for truly would I speak,

Cheered on with a hunting horn heard In Crete, Sparte, or Thessaly: You can judge so when you hear them. But wait, who are these people?

My lord, this is my daughter Hermia, fast asleep, And this is Lysander, and this is Demetrius, And this is Helena, Nedar's daughter. I wonder why they are all here together.

They must have woken early in order to keep The rites of May Day, and, knowing my plans to celebrate it as well, Came here to join us. But Egeus: isn't today the day When Hermia must tell us how she answers?

Yes, it is, my lord.

Go, and tell the huntsmen to blow their horns to wake them.

Horns and shout within. LYSANDER, DEMETRIUS, HELENA, and HERMIA wake and start up

Good morning, friends. Valentine's day is past: Shouldn't you lovebirds have paired up back then?

Forgive us, my lord.

Please, all of you stand up. I know you two, Lysander and Demetrius, are rivals, So how is there this peace in the world And how in your jealousy did you not hate each other, To the point where you could sleep next to each other and not be afraid of wrongdoing?

My lord, I am rather confused, but I will reply In my half-sleep, half-woken state. So far, I promise, I don't really know how I came here. But I think, -- well I want to tell you the truth

And now do I bethink me, so it is,--
I came with Hermia hither: our intent
Was to be gone from Athens, where we might,
Without the peril of the Athenian law.

EGEUS
Enough, enough, my lord; you have enough:
I beg the law, the law, upon his head.
They would have stolen away; they would,
Demetrius,
Thereby to have defeated you and me,
You of your wife and me of my consent,
Of my consent that she should be your wife.

DEMETRIUS
My lord, fair Helen told me of their stealth,
Of this their purpose hither to this wood;
And I in fury hither follow'd them,
Fair Helena in fancy following me.
But, my good lord, I wot not by what power,--
But by some power it is,--my love to Hermia,
Melted as the snow, seems to me now
As the remembrance of an idle gaud
Which in my childhood I did dote upon;
And all the faith, the virtue of my heart,
The object and the pleasure of mine eye,
Is only Helena. To her, my lord,
Was I betroth'd ere I saw Hermia:
But, like in sickness, did I loathe this food;
But, as in health, come to my natural taste,
Now I do wish it, love it, long for it,
And will for evermore be true to it.

THESEUS
Fair lovers, you are fortunately met:
Of this discourse we more will hear anon.
Egeus, I will overbear your will;
For in the temple by and by with us
These couples shall eternally be knit:
And, for the morning now is something worn,
Our purposed hunting shall be set aside.
Away with us to Athens; three and three,
We'll hold a feast in great solemnity.
Come, Hippolyta.

*And now that I think about it, I think this is true
-- I came here with Hermia, in order to
Run away from Athens, to wherever we could,
So that we would not have to face the dangers of
the Athenian law.*

*My lord, you've heard enough already:
Now I beg you to enforce the law and punish
him. They would have run away, they would
have, Demetrius,
And thus would have defeated both of us,
Stealing your wife, and my consent,
My consent that Hermia should be your wife.*

*My lord, Helena told me of their plans
And their purpose for coming to the forest,
And I furiously followed them,
Beautiful Helena, out of love for me, following
me. But, my lord, I do not know what power
changed me -- Though it is certainly a strong
power -- but this power changed my love for
Hermia, And melted it away, like snow, so that
now I remember it as a worthless trinket That I
loved when I was still a child. And now, all of
my heart and soul finds As its sole pleasure
Only Helena. I was, my lord,
Meant to marry her before I ever saw Hermia,
But as if I were sick and rejecting good food, I
rejected this too. Now I am healthy and returned
to my natural tastes, And I wish for, love, and
long for Helena, And will forevermore be
faithful to her.*

*Fair lovers, it is fortunate we met here.
We will hear more about this soon.
Egeus, I must override your request:
In the temple with Hippolyta and me
These two couples will be wed for eternity.
And as the morning is almost passed,
We will put our hunting trip on hold for another
time. Let us go to Athens now: three men and
three women to marry, Well we will have a great
feast together. Let us go, Hippolyta.*

Exeunt THESEUS, HIPPOLYTA, EGEUS, and train

69

DEMETRIUS

These things seem small and undistinguishable,
Like far-off mountains turnèd into clouds.

*Everything from last night looks small, and hard
to make out, Like a mountain far away that
looks like distant clouds.*

HERMIA

Methinks I see these things with parted eye,
When every thing seems double.

*I feel like I see the everything as blurry,
Or in double vision.*

HELENA

So methinks:
And I have found Demetrius like a jewel,
Mine own, and not mine own.

*Yes, me too.
I feel like Demetrius is a jewel I have found,
And is thus mine, but also not mine, that
someone else could claim him at any time.*

DEMETRIUS

Are you sure
That we are awake? It seems to me
That yet we sleep, we dream. Do not you think
The duke was here, and bid us follow him?

*Is it certain
That we are all awake? It feels like
We are still asleep and dreaming. Was the duke
Really here, and did he ask us to follow him?*

HERMIA

Yea; and my father.

Yes, my father was here as well.

HELENA

And Hippolyta.

And Hippolyta.

LYSANDER

And he did bid us follow to the temple.

And he asked us to go to the temple with him.

DEMETRIUS

Why, then, we are awake: let's follow him
And by the way let us recount our dreams.

*Well we are definitely awake, then. Let's follow
Duke Theseus And tell each other our dreams as
we walk.*

Exeunt

BOTTOM

[Awaking] When my cue comes, call me, and I will
answer: my next is, 'Most fair Pyramus.' Heigh-ho!
Peter Quince! Flute, the bellows-mender! Snout,
the tinker! Starveling! God's my life, stolen
hence, and left me asleep! I have had a most rare
vision. I have had a dream, past the wit of man to
say what dream it was: man is but an ass, if he go

*Tell me when it is my cue and I will
say my line — the next one is "Most fair
Pyramus." Hello!
Peter Quince! Flute, the bellows-repairman!
Snout,
The repairman! Starveling! My God, they have
left while I was asleep! I had the strangest
dream. It is outside of the abilities of mankind
to explain it: a man is as foolish as a donkey if
he tries to
explain the dream of mine. I thought I was --*

about to expound this dream. Methought I was--
there
is no man can tell what. Methought I was,--and
methought I had,--but man is but a patched fool,
if
he will offer to say what methought I had. The
eye
of man hath not heard, the ear of man hath not
seen, man's hand is not able to taste, his tongue
to conceive, nor his heart to report, what my
dream
was. I will get Peter Quince to write a ballad of
this dream: it shall be called Bottom's Dream,
because it hath no bottom; and I will sing it in
the
latter end of a play, before the duke:
peradventure, to make it the more gracious, I
shall
sing it at her death.

well no one can really say what exactly. I
thought I was -- and I
thought I had -- but someone would be an idiot
to
say what I thought I had. A man's eye
has not heard, his ear has not
seen, his hand cannot taste, and his tongue
cannot touch, nor his heart explain, what my
dream
was. I will ask Peter Quince to write a ballad
song
about my dream and will call it "Bottom's
Dream,"
because it doesn't have a bottom, and I will sing
it
at the end of the play, in front of the duke.
In fact, to make it even more lovely, I will
sing it when Thisby dies.

Exit

Scene II

Athens. QUINCE'S house.

Enter QUINCE, FLUTE, SNOUT, and STARVELING

QUINCE
Have you sent to Bottom's house ? is he come
home yet?

Have you been to Bottom's house? Is he home yet?

STARVELING
He cannot be heard of. Out of doubt he is
transported.

No one has heard anything. I'm certain he has been taken.

FLUTE
If he come not, then the play is marred: it goes
not forward, doth it?

If he does not come, then the play is ruined – it can't go forward, right?

QUINCE
It is not possible: you have not a man in all
Athens able to discharge Pyramus but he.

It's impossible – no one in all of Athens can play Pyramus convincingly except for Bottom.

FLUTE
No, he hath simply the best wit of any handicraft
man in Athens.

I agree – he is the smartest of all handymen in Athens.

QUINCE
Yea and the best person too; and he is a very
paramour for a sweet voice.

Yes, and the best looking man, as well. And he is a very paramour for a sweet voice.

FLUTE
You must say 'paragon:' a paramour is, God
bless us,
a thing of naught.

You mean "paragon," a paramour is something bad.

Enter SNUG

SNUG
Masters, the duke is coming from the temple,
and
there is two or three lords and ladies more
married:
if our sport had gone forward, we had all been
made
men.

*Everyone, the duke is leaving the temple, and two or three more men and women were married.
If we could have performed our play, we would have been rich men.*

FLUTE
O sweet bully Bottom! Thus hath he lost

Oh that Bottom! He has not lost getting paid

72

sixpence a
day during his life; he could not have 'scaped
sixpence a day: an the duke had not given him
sixpence a day for playing Pyramus, I'll be
hanged;
he would have deserved it: sixpence a day in
Pyramus, or nothing.

sixpence
every day of his life, I'm sure he would have
been forced to take sixpence a day, and if the
duke would not have given him sixpence a day
for his performance of Pyramus, I would have
hung myself. Bottom would have deserved
sixpence a day to play Pyramus, or it's nothing.

Enter BOTTOM

BOTTOM
Where are these lads? where are these hearts?

Where are you boys, where are you friends?

QUINCE
Bottom! O most courageous day! O most happy
hour!

Bottom! Oh great timing, what a wonderful day!

BOTTOM
Masters, I am to discourse wonders: but ask me
not
what; for if I tell you, I am no true Athenian. I
will tell you every thing, right as it fell out.

Friends, I have many odd things to tell you, but
do not
ask me what they are. If I tell you, I am not an
Athenian, and so I won't. Or I will tell you
everything, just as it happened.

QUINCE
Let us hear, sweet Bottom.

Please tell us, Bottom.

BOTTOM
Not a word of me. All that I will tell you is, that
the duke hath dined. Get your apparel together,
good strings to your beards, new ribbons to your
pumps; meet presently at the palace; every man
look
o'er his part; for the short and the long is, our
play is preferred. In any case, let Thisby have
clean linen; and let not him that plays the lion
pair his nails, for they shall hang out for the
lion's claws. And, most dear actors, eat no
onions
nor garlic, for we are to utter sweet breath; and I
do not doubt but to hear them say, it is a sweet
comedy. No more words: away! go, away!

I will not tell you a single word except that
the duke has eaten. Get your costumes together,
tie the beards on with good strings, and put new
ribbons on your shows. We must go immediately
to the palace. Everyone
look over your lines because, basically, the duke
wants to hear our play. Anyway, give Thisby the
clean clothes and do not clip the nails of him
who plays the lion, for they should look like
lion claws. Oh, and actors: do not eat onions
or garlic, because our breath should smell good.
I am sure they will all say that ours is a pleasant
and sweet comedy. I have nothing else to say,
now go, get ready!

Exeunt

Act V

Athens. The palace of THESEUS.

Enter THESEUS, HIPPOLYTA, PHILOSTRATE, Lords and Attendants

HIPPOLYTA
'Tis strange my Theseus, that these
lovers speak of.

*It's a strange story, Theseus, that these
lovers tell.*

THESEUS
More strange than true: I never may believe
These antique fables, nor these fairy toys.
Lovers and madmen have such seething brains,
Such shaping fantasies, that apprehend
More than cool reason ever comprehends.
The lunatic, the lover and the poet
Are of imagination all compact:
One sees more devils than vast hell can hold,
That is, the madman: the lover, all as frantic,
Sees Helen's beauty in a brow of Egypt:
The poet's eye, in fine frenzy rolling,
Doth glance from heaven to earth, from earth to
heaven;
And as imagination bodies forth
The forms of things unknown, the poet's pen
Turns them to shapes and gives to airy nothing
A local habitation and a name.
Such tricks hath strong imagination,
That if it would but apprehend some joy,
It comprehends some bringer of that joy;
Or in the night, imagining some fear,
How easy is a bush supposed a bear!

*More strange than it is true, I think. I will never
believe These old tales or fairy stories.
Both lovers and madmen are able to
Hallucinate and see such things, things
That cool, collected reason would never see.
The crazy person, lover, and poet
Share heightened imaginations:
One sees demons everywhere, more than are
even in hell, And that is the crazy person. The
lover, just as crazy, Sees unimaginable beauty,
like that of ancient Helen, in an Egyptian's face.
And the poet, in a frenzy, Looks from heaven to
earth, and from earth to heaven,
And just as imagination creates in one's mind
The form of things that do not exist, the poet by
writing Describes their shapes and gives a name
And a place things that are really nothing.
These people have such strong imaginations
That if they think of some joy they want,
They then believe that that joy has arrived.
Or, at nighttime, they might imagine something
scary And believe that the bush is a bear!*

HIPPOLYTA
But all the story of the night told over,
And all their minds transfigured so together,
More witnesseth than fancy's images
And grows to something of great constancy;
But, howsoever, strange and admirable.

*But the story these lovers are telling of the night,
And how they all say the same things,
Seems to point to more than just imagined
images And becomes something very consistent
– But whatever the truth, it is a story both
strange and interesting.*

THESEUS
Here come the lovers, full of joy and mirth.

Here come the lovers, happy and joyful.

Enter LYSANDER, DEMETRIUS, HERMIA, and HELENA

Joy, gentle friends! joy and fresh days of love
Accompany your hearts!

Joy to you, my friends! I wish joy and days full of love for your hearts!

LYSANDER
More than to us
Wait in your royal walks, your board, your bed!

*We wish you more joy, which
Will be with you in your royal walks, your dinner table, and your bed!*

THESEUS
Come now; what masques, what dances shall we have,
To wear away this long age of three hours
Between our after-supper and bed-time?
Where is our usual manager of mirth?
What revels are in hand? Is there no play,
To ease the anguish of a torturing hour?
Call Philostrate.

*Now what dances and performances will we have
In order to fill the three hours
Between our dinner and our bedtime?
Where is the one who manages the entertainment? What fun is in store for us? Isn't there a play To fill this torturous boredom?
Call Philostrate to me.*

PHILOSTRATE
Here, mighty Theseus.

I am here, mighty Theseus.

THESEUS
Say, what abridgement have you for this evening?
What masque? what music? How shall we beguile
The lazy time, if not with some delight?

*Tell me, what entertainment did you plan for the evening?
What play or music? How will we pass
This lazy time if now with something fun?*

PHILOSTRATE
There is a brief how many sports are ripe:
Make choice of which your highness will see first.

*Here is a list of what entertainment is available:
Choice whichever your highness would like first.*

Giving a paper

THESEUS
[Reads] 'The battle with the Centaurs, to be sung
By an Athenian eunuch to the harp.'
We'll none of that: that have I told my love,
In glory of my kinsman Hercules.

"The battle between Hercules and the Centaurs, sung By an Athenian eunuch while playing the harp." Not that one: I told that story to Hippolyta To praise my friend Hercules.

Reads

'The riot of the tipsy Bacchanals,
Tearing the Thracian singer in their rage.'

*"The riots of the drunken Bacchanals
Who rip apart the singer from Thrace, Orpheus,*

That is an old device; and it was play'd
When I from Thebes came last a conqueror.

'The thrice three Muses mourning for the death
Of Learning, late deceased in beggary.'
That is some satire, keen and critical,
Not sorting with a nuptial ceremony.

'A tedious brief scene of young Pyramus
And his love Thisbe; very tragical mirth.'
Merry and tragical! tedious and brief!
That is, hot ice and wondrous strange snow.
How shall we find the concord of this discord?

PHILOSTRATE
A play there is, my lord, some ten words long,
Which is as brief as I have known a play;
But by ten words, my lord, it is too long,
Which makes it tedious; for in all the play
There is not one word apt, one player fitted:
And tragical, my noble lord, it is;
For Pyramus therein doth kill himself.
Which, when I saw rehearsed, I must confess,
Made mine eyes water; but more merry tears
The passion of loud laughter never shed.

THESEUS
What are they that do play it?

PHILOSTRATE
Hard-handed men that work in Athens here,
Which never labour'd in their minds till now,
And now have toil'd their unbreathed memories
With this same play, against your nuptial.

THESEUS
And we will hear it.

PHILOSTRATE
No, my noble lord;
It is not for you: I have heard it over,

in their rage." This is an old tale: I saw it
When I came from Thebes as a conqueror.

Reads

"Nine Muses mourning for the death
Of Learning and Knowledge, deceased after
being poor." This seems to be a satire, very
analytical, And not matching the mood of a
wedding ceremony.

Reads

A tedious brief scene of young Pyramus
And his love Thisbe; very sad happiness."
Happy and sad! Tedious, but still brief!
That's like hot ice, and strange snow.
What is the harmony to this disharmony? How
do these things fit together?

Yes, that is a play, my lord, of about ten words
long, As brief as any play I have ever known.
But these ten words are ten too many,
Which makes the play tedious. In the whole play,
Not a single word is the right one, nor one actor
adept. Tragic and sad, my lord, it certainly is,
For Pyramus kills himself in the play.
This event, when I saw it rehearsed, I must be
honest, Made me cry – but happier tears
Has my loud laughter never cried like these.

Who are the actors?

Common workers and handymen in Athens,
Who never tried working their minds until now,
And now have overworked their minds
With this play for your wedding.

Then we will hear it.

No, my noble lord,
This is not the play for you. I have heard it

And it is nothing, nothing in the world;
Unless you can find sport in their intents,
Extremely stretch'd and conn'd with cruel pain,
To do you service.

THESEUS
I will hear that play;
For never anything can be amiss,
When simpleness and duty tender it.
Go, bring them in: and take your places, ladies.

HIPPOLYTA
I love not to see wretchedness o'er charged
And duty in his service perishing.

THESEUS
Why, gentle sweet, you shall see no such thing.

HIPPOLYTA
He says they can do nothing in this kind.

THESEUS
The kinder we, to give them thanks for nothing.
Our sport shall be to take what they mistake:
And what poor duty cannot do, noble respect
Takes it in might, not merit.
Where I have come, great clerks have purposed
To greet me with premeditated welcomes;
Where I have seen them shiver and look pale,
Make periods in the midst of sentences,
Throttle their practised accent in their fears
And in conclusion dumbly have broke off,
Not paying me a welcome. Trust me, sweet,
Out of this silence yet I pick'd a welcome;
And in the modesty of fearful duty
I read as much as from the rattling tongue
Of saucy and audacious eloquence.
Love, therefore, and tongue-tied simplicity
In least speak most, to my capacity.

And it is worth nothing, nothing at all, Unless you would enjoy watching their attempts to perform, Their bad acting and the memorization that must have cost them much pain, And then it might suit you.

That is the play I want, Since nothing can be wrong When simple people try and work hard in something. Bring them in front of us. Ladies, take your seats.

Exit PHILOSTRATE

I do not like to see poor people asked to go above their capabilities And fail in their attempts to do something right.

Why, my dear, you will not see such a thing.

Philostrate says they cannot act or perform well at all.

Then we are kind to thank them for giving us nothing. It will be fun to accept their mistakes, And anyway, noble people should judge what duty and hard work cannot accomplish By its attempts, not by its artistic merit. I have traveled to places where brilliant thinkers have tried To greet me with planned out and memorized speeches, And time after time I watched them get nervous and become pale, Stutter and stop in the middle of their sentences, Mess up their formal tones from being afraid, And finally end their speeches prematurely, In the end not even welcoming me. Trust me, From their silence and awkwardness I still saw their intent to welcome me, And in their humbleness that made them afraid, I saw just as much of a welcoming speech as I do from those who speak easily And give creative, loud, eloquent speeches. Thus, someone who loves but still falters in their simple speech Means most to me and can say the most, even when saying the least.

PHILOSTRATE
So please your grace, the Prologue is address'd.

THESEUS
Let him approach.

Prologue
If we offend, it is with our good will.
That you should think, we come not to offend,
But with good will. To show our simple skill,
That is the true beginning of our end.
Consider then we come but in despite.
We do not come as minding to contest you,
Our true intent is. All for your delight
We are not here. That you should here repent you,
The actors are at hand and by their show
You shall know all that you are like to know.

THESEUS
This fellow doth not stand upon points.

LYSANDER
He hath rid his prologue like a rough colt; he knows
not the stop. A good moral, my lord: it is not
enough to speak, but to speak true.

HIPPOLYTA
Indeed he hath played on his prologue like a child
on a recorder; a sound, but not in government.

THESEUS
His speech, was like a tangled chain; nothing
impaired, but all disordered. Who is next?

Prologue (QUINCE)
Gentles, perchance you wonder at this show;
But wonder on, till truth make all things plain.

Re-enter PHILOSTRATE

If you are ready, my grace, the prologue is ready to be given.

Let him start.
Flourish of trumpets

Enter QUINCE for the Prologue

If we offend you, know that we offend you out of our desire to. Or, in other words, we haven't come to offend you, But we came to bother you most with our good intentions. To show the talent of our performance This is the beginning of our deaths. Recognize that we are coming here in spite of. We do not come here to make you oppose you, Our true goal. For your happiness, We didn't come. That you should be forced to apologize, The actors are ready to make you do that, and from the play You will find out everything you are meant to know.

This man doesn't see the actual punctuation.

He read the prologue like one riding an unbroken horse, not knowing when to stop. A good lesson, my lord: just speaking is not good enough – it is also important to speak well, with good grammar.

Yes, he spoke that prologue like a child playin a recorder – all sounds with no coherence.

His speech was like a knotted and tangled chain: nothing was wrong with the actual speech, but the parts were all jumbled. Who is next?

Enter Pyramus and Thisbe, Wall, Moonshine, and Lion

Gentlemen and ladies, you might be confused at this play, But continue to think on it and

This man is Pyramus, if you would know;
This beauteous lady Thisby is certain.
This man, with lime and rough-cast, doth present
Wall, that vile Wall which did these lovers sunder;
And through Wall's chink, poor souls, they are content
To whisper. At the which let no man wonder.
This man, with lanthorn, dog, and bush of thorn,
Presenteth Moonshine; for, if you will know,
By moonshine did these lovers think no scorn
To meet at Ninus' tomb, there, there to woo.
This grisly beast, which Lion hight by name,
The trusty Thisby, coming first by night,
Did scare away, or rather did affright;
And, as she fled, her mantle she did fall,
Which Lion vile with bloody mouth did stain.
Anon comes Pyramus, sweet youth and tall,
And finds his trusty Thisby's mantle slain:
Whereat, with blade, with bloody blameful blade,
He bravely broach'd is boiling bloody breast;
And Thisby, tarrying in mulberry shade,
His dagger drew, and died. For all the rest,
Let Lion, Moonshine, Wall, and lovers twain
At large discourse, while here they do remain.

THESEUS
I wonder if the lion be to speak.

DEMETRIUS
No wonder, my lord: one lion may, when many asses do.

WALL
In this same interlude it doth befall
That I, one Snout by name, present a wall;
And such a wall, as I would have you think,
That had in it a crannied hole or chink,
Through which the lovers, Pyramus and Thisby,
Did whisper often very secretly.
This loam, this rough-cast and this stone doth show

everything will be clear. This man is Pyramus,
And this beautiful lady is Thisby.
This man covered with cement and gravel is
the Wall, the evil Wall which separated the lovers
who, through a small hole in the Wall, they had to
whisper. So that should clear up his part.
And this man, with the lantern, dog, and thornbush,
Is playing the Moonshine – since, you know,
It was by the moon that these lovers without
shame met at Ninus' tomb, in order to court.
This ugly animal, which we call a lion,
Saw Thisby, after she came to the tomb on the
first night, And scared her away, and frightened
her severely. As she ran away, her cloak fell off
And the evil Lion chewed on it with an already
bloody mouth. Quickly after came Pyramus, a
tall and handsome youth, Who saw Thisby's
cloak bloodied, And, with his bloody, angry
sword,
He bravely thrust it into his chest.
Thisby, hiding in the shade of a mulberry tree
Saw this and took Pyramus' dagger, and kill
herself. For the rest of the story I will let Lion,
Moonshine, Wall, and the two lovers Speak
about it, since they are right here.

Exeunt Prologue, Thisbe, Lion, and Moonshine

I wonder if the lion will speak.

Why not? Why shouldn't one lion speak when
these donkeys have already.

At this time, it is worth repeating
That I am playing a wall (my real name is
Snout). The wall I am portraying, please believe,
Has a hole in it
That the lovers Pyramus and Thisby
Whisper through secretly.
This stone and gravel all around me should
make it clear

That I am that same wall; the truth is so:
And this the cranny is, right and sinister,
Through which the fearful lovers are to whisper.

That I am that wall, and truly,
The hole is right here, each side of it,
And through it the lovers will whisper.

THESEUS
Would you desire lime and hair to speak better?

Can cement ever speak better?

DEMETRIUS
It is the wittiest partition that ever I heard
discourse, my lord.

It is the smartest room divider that I have ever
heard converse, my lord.

Enter Pyramus

THESEUS
Pyramus draws near the wall: silence!

Pyramus is going near the wall, be quiet!

PYRAMUS
O grim-look'd night! O night with hue so black!
O night, which ever art when day is not!
O night, O night! alack, alack, alack,
I fear my Thisby's promise is forgot!
And thou, O wall, O sweet, O lovely wall,
That stand'st between her father's ground and
mine!
Thou wall, O wall, O sweet and lovely wall,
Show me thy chink, to blink through with mine
eyne!

Thanks, courteous wall: Jove shield thee well
for this!
But what see I? No Thisby do I see.
O wicked wall, through whom I see no bliss!
Cursed be thy stones for thus deceiving me!

Oh night that looks so grim and black!
Oh night, which is always there when the day is
not! Oh night, oh night! I am so sad, so sad,
Because I am afraid Thisby forgot her promise!
And you, oh sweet and wonderful wall,
You stand between her father's property and
mine!
You, sweet and wonderful wall, dear wall,
Show me the hole that I can look through with
my eye!
Wall holds up his fingers
Thank you, kind wall. God protect you for this!
But what do I see? Not Thisby.
Oh evil wall, I cannot see my happiness through
you!
Damn your stones for tricking me!

THESEUS
The wall, methinks, being sensible, should curse
again.

Since it is a speaking wall, it should reply to
Pyramus with a curse.

PYRAMUS
No, in truth, sir, he should not. 'Deceiving me'
is Thisby's cue: she is to enter now, and I am to
spy her through the wall. You shall see, it will
fall pat as I told you. Yonder she comes.

Not really, my lord, he shouldn't because
"Deceiving me" is the cue for Thisby to enter so
that I can see her through the wall. You'll see,
everything will happen like I said. Here she
comes.

Enter Thisbe

THISBE

O wall, full often hast thou heard my moans,
For parting my fair Pyramus and me!
My cherry lips have often kiss'd thy stones,
Thy stones with lime and hair knit up in thee.

Oh wall, you have heard my sad moans so often, blaming you For separating Pyramus and me! I have often kissed your stones with my lips as red as cherries, Your stones, stuck together with cement.

PYRAMUS

I see a voice: now will I to the chink,
To spy an I can hear my Thisby's face. Thisby!

I see something, now I will go to the hole And see if I can hear Thisby's face. Thisby!

THRISBE

My love thou art, my love I think.

You are my love, I think.

PYRAMUS

Think what thou wilt, I am thy lover's grace;
And, like Limander, am I trusty still.

Think whatever you want, I am your love: Just as faithful as heroic Limander.

THISBE

And I like Helen, till the Fates me kill.

And I will be as faithful as Helen of Troy, until the Fates decide my death.

PYRAMUS

Not Shafalus to Procrus was so true.

Not even Shafalus was as faithful to Procus.

THISBE

As Shafalus to Procrus, I to you.

Yes, I am like Shafalus to Procrus to you too.

PYRAMUS

O kiss me through the hole of this vile wall!

Oh kiss me through the hole of this evil wall!

THISBE

I kiss the wall's hole, not your lips at all.

I can only kiss the hole in the wall, I can't get to your lips.

PYRAMUS

Wilt thou at Ninny's tomb meet me straightway?

Then will you come meet me at Ninny's tomb right now?

THISBE

'Tide life, 'tide death, I come without delay.

I will come at once, and neither life nor death can stop me.

Exeunt Pyramus and Thisbe

WALL

Thus have I, Wall, my part discharged so;
And, being done, thus Wall away doth go.

Thus, I as Wall have finished my part, And since I am done, Wall will leave as well.

Exit

THESEUS
Now is the mural down between the two
neighbours.

*And now the wall is down that separated the
lovers.*

DEMETRIUS
No remedy, my lord, when walls are so wilful to
hear
without warning.

*There's nothing to do about it, lord, when walls
will hear and speak
without warning.*

HIPPOLYTA
This is the silliest stuff that ever I heard.

This is the silliest play I've ever heard.

THESEUS
The best in this kind are but shadows; and the
worst
are no worse, if imagination amend them.

*The best plays are just illusions of reality, and
so the worst
are not really worse – you just need imagination
to fix them.*

HIPPOLYTA
It must be your imagination then, and not theirs.

*But it must be the audience's imagination,
instead of the performers.*

THESEUS
If we imagine no worse of them than they of
themselves, they may pass for excellent men.
Here
come two noble beasts in, a man and a lion.

*If we imagine them as they think
of themselves, then they will look like the best of
all men. Here
come two very noble beasts: a man and a lion.*

Enter Lion and Moonshine

LION
You, ladies, you, whose gentle hearts do fear
The smallest monstrous mouse that creeps on
floor,
May now perchance both quake and tremble
here,
When lion rough in wildest rage doth roar.
Then know that I, one Snug the joiner, am
A lion-fell, nor else no lion's dam;
For, if I should as lion come in strife
Into this place, 'twere pity on my life.

*Dear ladies, whose gentle hears might be afraid
Of the smallest mouse creeping along the floor,
You might now be tremble with fear,
After an angry lion roars.
Please know that I am really Snug the wood
worker,
not really a fierce lion or a lioness.
If I were a lion, and came angrily
To this place, I would be giving up my life.*

THESEUS
A very gentle beast, of a good conscience.

What a kind beast, very caring for others.

DEMETRIUS
The very best at a beast, my lord, that e'er I saw.

*The best actor I've ever seen portray a lion, my
lord.*

LYSANDER

This lion is a very fox for his valour.

This lion is as brave as a fox.

THESEUS
True; and a goose for his discretion.

And as wise as a goose.

DEMETRIUS
Not so, my lord; for his valour cannot carry his discretion; and the fox carries the goose.

No, my lord, because his courage doesn't make him wiser – as would be suggested since a fox carries a goose.

THESEUS
His discretion, I am sure, cannot carry his valour;
for the goose carries not the fox. It is well: leave it to his discretion, and let us listen to the moon.

*Well his wisdom certainly can't carry his courage,
which makes sense, since the goose can't carry the fox. Well, we will leave the matter to his wisdom to resolve. I want to hear the moon.*

MOONSHINE
This lanthorn doth the horned moon present;--

This lantern is the crescent moon above--

DEMETRIUS
He should have worn the horns on his head.

Then he should have worn horns on his head.

THESEUS
He is no crescent, and his horns are invisible within the circumference.

This is no crescent moon, unless the horns are invisible within the moon itself.

MOONSHINE
This lanthorn doth the horned moon present;
Myself the man i' the moon do seem to be.

*This lantern is the crescent moon above
And I am the man in the moon.*

THESEUS
This is the greatest error of all the rest: the man should be put into the lanthorn. How is it else the
man i' the moon?

*They certainly made a mistake here: the actor should have been placed inside the lantern. How else would he be
the man in the moon?*

DEMETRIUS
He dares not come there for the candle; for, you see, it is already in snuff.

He cannot go in there because of the candle; it is already charred and smoking.

HIPPOLYTA
I am aweary of this moon: would he would change!

I am tired of this moon and want it to change phases.

THESEUS
It appears, by his small light of discretion, that

It looks like, since he is not very bright,

he is in the wane; but yet, in courtesy, in all reason, we must stay the time.

he is waning, but we should be polite and see for certain.

LYSANDER
Proceed, Moon.

Continue, Moon.

MOONSHINE
All that I have to say, is, to tell you that the lanthorn is the moon; I, the man in the moon; this
thorn-bush, my thorn-bush; and this dog, my dog.

All I have to say is that the lantern is the moon, I am the man in the moon, this bush of thorns is mine, and this dog is mine.

DEMETRIUS
Why, all these should be in the lanthorn; for all these are in the moon. But, silence! here comes Thisbe.

Well all of these things should be inside the lantern then, since they are in the moon. But wait! here comes Thisbe.

Enter Thisbe

THISBE
This is old Ninny's tomb. Where is my love?

This is old Ninny's tomb, but where is Pyramus, my love?

LION
[Roaring] Oh--

Roar!

Thisbe runs off

DEMETRIUS
Well roared, Lion.

Great roaring, Lion.

THESEUS
Well run, Thisbe.

Great running, Thisbe.

HIPPOLYTA
Well shone, Moon. Truly, the moon shines with a
good grace.

Great shining, Moon. Really, the moon shines very beautifully.

The Lion shakes Thisbe's mantle

THESEUS
Well moused, Lion.

Well shaken, like a cat shaking a mouse, Lion.

DEMETRIUS
And then came Pyramus.

And now Pyramus enters.

Enter Pyramus

LYSANDER

And so the lion vanished.

And the lion is gone.

Exit Lion

PYRAMUS

Sweet Moon, I thank thee for thy sunny beams;
I thank thee, Moon, for shining now so bright;
For, by thy gracious, golden, glittering gleams,
I trust to take of truest Thisby sight.
But stay, O spite!
But mark, poor knight,
What dreadful dole is here!
Eyes, do you see?
How can it be?
O dainty duck! O dear!
Thy mantle good,
What, stain'd with blood!
Approach, ye Furies fell!
O Fates, come, come,
Cut thread and thrum;
Quail, crush, conclude, and quell!

Dear Moon, thank you for your bright beams,
Thank you for shining so brightly right now,
Because by your golden and shimmering beams
I can see Thisby even better.
But wait, Oh no!
What is this, poor me,
What is this awful thing!
Eyes, do you see what it is?
How is it possible?
Oh dainty duck! Oh dear!
Your good cloak
is what, it is stained with blood!
Come you Furies, and avenge me!
Come you Fates, come,
And cut the thread of my life,
Crush, finish, kill!

THESEUS

This passion, and the death of a dear friend,
would
go near to make a man look sad.

Such passion of an actor, next to the death of a
close friend,
could make someone very sad while watching
this.

HIPPOLYTA

Beshrew my heart, but I pity the man.

I blame my heart, but I actually feel sorry for
this man.

PYRAMUS

O wherefore, Nature, didst thou lions frame?
Since lion vile hath here deflower'd my dear:
Which is--no, no--which was the fairest dame
That lived, that loved, that liked, that look'd with
cheer.
Come, tears, confound;
Out, sword, and wound
The pap of Pyramus;
Ay, that left pap,
Where heart doth hop:

Oh Nature, why did you create lions?
An evil lion has eaten my love
Who is – no – who was the most beautiful
woman
Who lived, loved, and was happy.
Come out tears, and overflow;
Come out sword, and hurt
My chest –
Yes, the left part of the chest
Where my heart beats.

Stabs himself

Thus die I, thus, thus, thus.
Now am I dead,

This is how I will die, like this, like this.
Now I am dead

Now am I fled;
My soul is in the sky:
Tongue, lose thy light;
Moon take thy flight:

And running from this life.
My soul is already in heaven.
Tongue, it is time to stop talking.
Moon, leave me in the dark.

Exit Moonshine

Now die, die, die, die, die.

Now I die, die, die, die, die.

Dies

DEMETRIUS
No die, but an ace, for him; for he is but one.

We may not have dice around, but he is a die with a single dot, since he is only one person.

LYSANDER
Less than an ace, man; for he is dead; he is
nothing.

Less than that even: since he is dead, he has no dots, he is nothing.

THESEUS
With the help of a surgeon he might yet recover,
and
prove an ass.

A doctor could perhaps help him and bring him back as a donkey.

HIPPOLYTA
How chance Moonshine is gone before Thisbe
comes
back and finds her lover?

Why is the Moon gone before Thisbe returns and finds Pyramus? How will she find him?

THESEUS
She will find him by starlight. Here she comes;
and
her passion ends the play.

By starlight, I suppose. Here she comes, and the play ends with her passion.

Re-enter Thisbe

HIPPOLYTA
Methinks she should not use a long one for such
a
Pyramus: I hope she will be brief.

I dont think Thisbe should grieve too long for such a ridiculous Pyramus, and I hope that she is quick.

DEMETRIUS
A mote will turn the balance, which Pyramus,
which
Thisbe, is the better; he for a man, God warrant
us;
she for a woman, God bless us.

So far it is even as to whether Pyramus or Thisbe is better. God help us if he is a better man, and God help us if she is a better woman.

LYSANDER
She hath spied him already with those sweet

She has already seen him with those pretty eyes.

eyes.

DEMETRIUS
And thus she means, videlicet:--

And, as follows, she will—

THISBE

Asleep, my love?	*My love, are you asleep?*
What, dead, my dove?	*Or are you dead?*
O Pyramus, arise!	*Pyramus get up!*
Speak, speak. Quite dumb?	*Please speak, can you not speak?*
Dead, dead? A tomb	*Are you really dead? In a tomb*
Must cover thy sweet eyes.	*You should be placed then, your beautiful eyes*
These My lips,	*closed. These lips of yours that were mine,*
This cherry nose,	*Your red nose*
These yellow cowslip cheeks,	*And your yellow cheeks like cowslip flowers,*
Are gone, are gone:	*Are gone!*
Lovers, make moan:	*Lovers, cry with me.*
His eyes were green as leeks.	*His eyes were green, like leeks.*
O Sisters Three,	*O Fates, the three Sisters,*
Come, come to me,	*Come to me*
With hands as pale as milk;	*With your pale hands*
Lay them in gore,	*And place them in the red gore of his body*
Since you have shore	*Since you have cut*
With shears his thread of silk.	*His life's thread with your scissors.*
Tongue, not a word:	*Tongue, be silent,*
Come, trusty sword;	*Come, sword of Pyramus,*
Come, blade, my breast imbrue:	*Come, blade, and enter my chest.*

Stabs herself

And, farewell, friends;	*Goodbye friends,*
Thus Thisby ends:	*Thus Thisby dies,*
Adieu, adieu, adieu.	*Goodbye, goodbye, goodbye.*

Dies

THESEUS
Moonshine and Lion are left to bury the dead.

So Moonshine and Lion must bury the bodies.

DEMETRIUS
Ay, and Wall too.

Yes, and Wall.

BOTTOM
[Starting up] No assure you; the wall is down that
parted their fathers. Will it please you to see the epilogue, or to hear a Bergomask dance between

No, really: the wall that parted them was taken down. Would you like to hear the epilogue, or hear and watch a dance from two

two
of our company?

THESEUS
No epilogue, I pray you; for your play needs no
excuse. Never excuse; for when the players are
all
dead, there needs none to be blamed. Marry, if
he
that writ it had played Pyramus and hanged
himself
in Thisbe's garter, it would have been a fine
tragedy: and so it is, truly; and very notably
discharged. But come, your Bergomask: let your
epilogue alone.

The iron tongue of midnight hath told twelve:
Lovers, to bed; 'tis almost fairy time.
I fear we shall out-sleep the coming morn
As much as we this night have overwatch'd.
This palpable-gross play hath well beguiled
The heavy gait of night. Sweet friends, to bed.
A fortnight hold we this solemnity,
In nightly revels and new jollity.

of our group?

*Please, no epilogue, the play doesn't need
an excuse. There's no point, anyway: since
everyone
is dead, no one needs to be blamed. Actually, if
you
had written that Pyramus had hanged himself
with Thisbe's belt, then it would have been a
great
tragedy. Anyway, it was still very well
done. Now, your dance – leave your
epilogue alone.*

A dance

*The bell is ringing out that it is midnight,
So lovers, head to your beds. It's time for the
fairies to come out. I am worried that we will
sleep in and miss the morning Since we have
been awake so late tonight. This incredibly
awful play has given a light air To the heaviness
of the night. My friends, let us go to bed. We will
continue this ceremony for two weeks, With
nightly parties and new entertainments.*

Exeunt

Scene II

Enter PUCK

PUCK

Now the hungry lion roars,	*Now the hungry lion roars*
And the wolf behowls the moon;	*And the wolf howls at the moon,*
Whilst the heavy ploughman snores,	*While the fat farmer snores*
All with weary task fordone.	*Tired from his work.*
Now the wasted brands do glow,	*The used up firewood glows in the fireplace*
Whilst the screech-owl, screeching loud,	*While the owl, screeching loudly,*
Puts the wretch that lies in woe	*Reminds the man who is sick*
In remembrance of a shroud.	*Of the shroud of impending death.*
Now it is the time of night	*Now is the time of the night*
That the graves all gaping wide,	*When the graves open*
Every one lets forth his sprite,	*And out of every one comes a ghost*
In the church-way paths to glide:	*To glide along the paths of the graveyard.*
And we fairies, that do run	*And we fairies, who follow*
By the triple Hecate's team,	*Hecate the goddess of magic,*
From the presence of the sun,	*And must run from the sun*
Following darkness like a dream,	*To follow darkness like a dream,*
Now are frolic: not a mouse	*Want to frolic. But for now not a single mouse*
Shall disturb this hallow'd house:	*Will disturb this special house.*
I am sent with broom before,	*I was sent with a broom*
To sweep the dust behind the door.	*To clean up everything for the king and queen.*

Enter OBERON and TITANIA with their train

OBERON

Through the house give gathering light,	*The house has a little light still*
By the dead and drowsy fire:	*From the dying fire.*
Every elf and fairy sprite	*All the elves and fairies with us,*
Hop as light as bird from brier;	*Walk lightly, like a bird stepping around thorns,*
And this ditty, after me,	*And sing this song with me,*
Sing, and dance it trippingly.	*Sing and dance joyfully.*

TITANIA

First, rehearse your song by rote	*First, rehearse your song by remembering*
To each word a warbling note:	*Each word and the note that goes with it.*
Hand in hand, with fairy grace,	*Now, join hands, and with the grace of fairies*
Will we sing, and bless this place.	*We will sing while we bless this house.*

Song and dance

OBERON

Now, until the break of day,	*Now, until morning,*
Through this house each fairy stray.	*Go through all the corners of the house.*

To the best bride-bed will we,
Which by us shall blessed be;
And the issue there create
Ever shall be fortunate.
So shall all the couples three
Ever true in loving be;
And the blots of Nature's hand
Shall not in their issue stand;
Never mole, hare lip, nor scar,
Nor mark prodigious, such as are
Despised in nativity,
Shall upon their children be.
With this field-dew consecrate,
Every fairy take his gait;
And each several chamber bless,
Through this palace, with sweet peace;
And the owner of it blest
Ever shall in safety rest.
Trip away; make no stay;
Meet me all by break of day.

PUCK

If we shadows have offended,
Think but this, and all is mended,
That you have but slumber'd here
While these visions did appear.
And this weak and idle theme,
No more yielding but a dream,
Gentles, do not reprehend:
if you pardon, we will mend:
And, as I am an honest Puck,
If we have unearned luck
Now to 'scape the serpent's tongue,
We will make amends ere long;
Else the Puck a liar call;
So, good night unto you all.
Give me your hands, if we be friends,
And Robin shall restore amends.

*Titania and I will go to the bed of Hippolyta and
Theseus And bless it,
And the children conceived there
Will always be fortunate and lucky.
In fact, all three couples will be fortunate
And always faithful to each other.
The flaws that Nature sometimes produces
Will not exist in their children:
No moles, no cleft lips or scars,
No abnormal markings that are
So ugly and hated at birth
Will ever appear on their children.
Take this dew from the fields,
Each one of you,
And bless each room
Throughout the palace with peace.
And the palace owner will be blessed
With safety.
Go along and don't take too long,
And meet me again at dawn.*

Exeunt OBERON, TITANIA, and train

*If we fairies have offended you,
Then it will help you to think
That you have fallen asleep here
When you saw these visions.
Consider this weak story
Only a dream,
Gentlemen and ladies, and do not be upset with
me. Forgive us and we will fix everything,
And, since I am an honest Puck,
If we have the good fortune
Not to be hissed at,
We will make it up to you before long –
Or, you can call me a liar.
Goodnight to you all.
If you are friends, clap for me,
And I will make it all up to you.*

23093759R00051

Printed in Poland
by Amazon Fulfillment
Poland Sp. z o.o., Wrocław